DATE DUE

MALICE

ALSO BY KEIGO HIGASHINO

The Devotion of Suspect X

Salvation of a Saint

MALICE

Keigo Higashino

Translated by Alexander O. Smith

with Elye Alexander

Minotaur Books

New York

MALICE. Copyright © 1996 by Keigo Higashino. Translation copyright © 2014 by Alexander O. Smith. All rights reserved. For information, address St. Martin's Press, 175 Fifth Avenue, New York, N.Y. 10010.

www.minotaurbooks.com

Library of Congress Cataloging-in-Publication Data

Higashino, Keigo, 1958–
    [Akui. English]
    Malice / Keigo Higashino ; translated by Alexander O. Smith. — First U.S. edition.
        pages cm
    ISBN 978-1-250-03560-8 (hardcover)
    ISBN 978-1-250-03561-5 (e-book)
    1. Police—Japan—Fiction.   2. Murder—Investigation—Japan—Fiction.
I. Smith, Alexander O., translator.   II. Title.
    PL852.I3625A5713 2014
    895.63'6—dc23

                                                    2014019885

Minotaur books may be purchased for educational, business, or promotional use. For information on bulk purchases, please contact Macmillan Corporate and Premium Sales Department at 1-800-221-7945, extension 5442, or write specialmarkets@macmillan.com.

First published in Japan as *Akui*, by Kodansha

First English Edition: October 2014

10   9   8   7   6   5   4   3   2   1

CONTENTS

MALICE

1
MURDER

OSAMU NONOGUCHI'S ACCOUNT

The incident took place on April 16, 1996, a Tuesday. I left my house at three thirty in the afternoon to go to Kunihiko Hidaka's place, which was only one station away by train. From the train station, you then had to take a bus, but even after adding in walking time, I could make the trip in twenty minutes.

I would often drop in on my friend for no particular reason; however, today was different. This time I had a purpose in mind. If I didn't go today, I might not have the chance to see him again for quite some time.

His house was in a residential development and was one of the many upscale houses on his street. Some of the others would even qualify as mansions. The area had been forest once, and many of the owners had kept some of the original trees as part of their landscaping. The beech trees and oaks were tall enough to cast shade on the road.

Though roads in this part of town weren't particularly narrow, they were all one-way. I guess that this was simply another indication of the residents' status.

I wasn't particularly surprised when, a few years ago, Hidaka bought a house in this neighborhood. Anyone in the area with any ambition at all dreamed of living here someday.

Hidaka's house wasn't one of the mansions, but it was

definitely large for a couple with no children. Though the peaked gables on the roof gave it a Japanese look, it had bay windows, an arch over the front door, and flower boxes hanging from the second-story windows that were clearly Western in design. The house was the result of the application of ideas from both husband and wife, I reckoned, although, considering the low brick wall around the house, the balance seemed skewed in the wife's favor. She once admitted to me that she always wanted to live in an old, European-style castle. His wife was odd like that.

Correction. His late wife.

I walked along the wall, which was laid so only the long sides of the bricks faced the street, and pressed the intercom button by the gate.

There was no answer. Then I noticed the Saab was missing from the driveway. *Guess he's stepped out,* I thought.

I was wondering how to pass the time while waiting for him to return when I remembered the cherry tree in Hidaka's garden. The buds had been about 30 percent open the last time I was there, which was ten days ago. I wondered how the buds were coming along.

I let myself in through the gate, figuring it wasn't too much of a transgression. The path to the front door split into two along the way, with the offshoot leading toward the south side of the house. I followed that one to the garden.

A number of the cherry blossoms had already fallen, but enough were left on the tree to make it worthwhile viewing. That is, it would have been, if it hadn't been for the woman, a woman I didn't know, standing in the garden, looking down at the ground. She was dressed casually, in jeans and a sweater, and had something white and crumpled in her hand.

"Hello?" I called out.

She seemed startled and looked up at me quickly. "Oh, I'm sorry." She showed me what was in her hand: a white hat. "The wind caught it and carried it into the garden. I didn't see anyone home—I'm sorry."

She looked to be in her late thirties. Eyes, nose, and mouth small and unremarkable. A plain-faced woman with an unhealthy cast to her skin. For a moment, I wondered about her story, if the wind had really been blowing hard enough to carry a hat.

"Is there something interesting on the ground there?" I asked.

She smiled. "The grass was growing in so nicely, I wondered how they were taking care of it."

"I wish I could tell you." I shrugged. "This is my friend's house."

She nodded. It seemed to me that she'd already realized I didn't live here. "Sorry for the intrusion," she said quickly, then walked past me to the front gate.

About five minutes later I heard a car pulling into the driveway. It was Hidaka. I walked around to the front door to see his navy-blue Saab backing into the garage. Hidaka noticed me standing there and nodded. In the passenger seat, his new wife, Rie, smiled and bowed her head.

"Sorry," he said, getting out of the car. "I just stepped out to do some last-minute shopping, and the traffic was terrible. Have you been waiting long?"

"I was enjoying your cherry blossoms."

"What's left of them."

"It's a beautiful tree."

He grinned. "Yeah, it's great when it's in bloom, but after that? It's a real pain in the ass. That tree's right next to my office window and you should see the caterpillars."

"Then it's lucky you won't be working here for a while."

"Anything to escape caterpillar hell. Come on inside. We still haven't packed all the cups so I can at least offer you some coffee."

We went in through the arched entryway.

Practically everything in the house was already boxed up. Even the paintings had disappeared from the walls.

"You almost done packing?" I asked.

"All but the office," Hidaka said. "Not that we did much of it ourselves. We had the moving company come in a few times."

"Where're you going to sleep tonight?"

"I made a reservation at a hotel. The Crown. Except, I might end up sleeping here anyway."

We went into his office. It was decent size and looked oddly vacant with just a computer, a desk, and a small bookshelf remaining.

"I take it you've got a deadline tomorrow?"

Hidaka frowned and nodded. "Yeah, it's the last in a series. I have to send it to my publisher by fax tonight, if you can believe that. That's why I haven't turned off the phones yet."

"How many pages do you have left to write?"

"Thirty or so. I'll make it."

We sat in a couple of chairs facing each other by the corner of the desk. Rie came in, bringing the coffee.

"I wonder how the weather is in Vancouver. It's got to be colder than here," I said to both of them.

"It's a completely different latitude, so it's definitely colder."

"But it's nice that it'll be cool in the summer," Rie added. "I never liked having to run the air-conditioning all the time."

"I'd like to think that a cool breeze through the office will help me get more work done, but we both know that's not going to happen," Hidaka said with a grin.

"You should definitely come visit us, Osamu. We'll take you on a tour," Rie offered.

"Thanks. I'll take you up on that."

"Please do." Rie bowed slightly. "I'll leave you two to it, then." She headed back downstairs.

Hidaka stood, coffee cup in hand, and went over to the window. "I'm glad I got to see the cherry tree in full bloom at least."

"Hey, if it blooms nice next year, I'll take a picture and send it to you in Canada. Do they have cherry trees over there?"

"No idea. I know there's none near the place I'll be living, at least." He took a sip of his coffee.

"That reminds me. There was a woman in your garden a little while ago, before you got here." At first, I'd been hesitant to tell him.

"Oh, yeah?" Hidaka frowned.

I told him about the woman, and his suspicious frown turned into a wry smile. "Did her face look like one of those round-headed, wooden *kokeshi* dolls?"

"Yeah, now that you mention it, it did." I laughed.

"Yeah, her last name's Niimi. Lives down the street. She

might look young, but she's definitely over forty. Rie thinks she's married, but that her husband works in another city and they have one of those distance-marriage arrangements."

"You seem to know her. Are you friends?"

"Hardly." He opened the window and closed the screen. A warm breeze blew in, carrying with it the smell of leaves. "Quite the opposite, actually. I believe she has a grudge against me."

"A grudge? What for?"

"A cat. Her cat died the other day. Apparently she found it lying by the road. When she took it to a veterinarian, he told her he thought it had been poisoned."

"What does that have to do with you?"

"She thinks I'm responsible. That I put out a poisoned meatball and her cat ate it."

"Seriously? Why would she think that?"

"Oh, that's the best part." Hidaka pulled a magazine off the bookshelf and opened it. "Take a look."

It was an essay, entitled "The Limits of Patience," and Hidaka's photo was next to the title. The essay was about a cat that had a habit of wandering onto the author's property and bothering him. Every morning, he found cat poop in the garden, pawprints on the hood of his car, and his potted plants shredded. He'd seen a white-and-brown-speckled cat around, knew it was the culprit, but could do nothing about it. He'd tried everything he could think of but nothing worked. An old wives' tale says that cats are afraid of their reflections, so, in desperation, he lined up plastic bottles filled with water in the hope that the cat would see itself in these makeshift mirrors and be scared away. But that didn't work at all. The gist of this short essay was that the limits of his patience were tested daily.

"And the deceased was a white-and-brown-speckled cat?" I asked.

"Something like that, yeah."

"I see. No wonder she thinks you're the culprit."

"Last week, she comes over with this dark look on her face. She didn't accuse me of poisoning her cat outright, but she implied it strongly. Rie told her she was crazy and sent her packing. I thought that was end of it . . . but if she's been snooping around in the garden, I must still be her prime suspect. She's probably looking for poisoned meatballs."

"Persistent, isn't she?"

"Oh, women like that always are."

"Doesn't she know you're moving to Canada?"

"Rie explained that we were moving to Vancouver in a week, so why would we worry about a cat we only had to deal with a little while longer? She may not look it, but when it comes to a fight, Rie can really dig in." Hidaka laughed deeply.

"Well, she has a point. I can't see any reason why you guys would bother to kill that cat."

For some reason, Hidaka didn't respond right away. He just grinned, looking out the window. He finished his coffee before saying, "I did do it, you know."

"Huh?" I said, unable to grasp his meaning immediately. "Did what?"

"I killed the cat. I killed it with poisoned meatballs that I put out in our garden. I didn't really think it would work, at least not as well as it did."

I thought he was pulling my leg until I saw his face. He

was smiling, but it wasn't the kind of smile that went with a joke.

"Where did you get the poisoned meatballs?"

"That part was easy. I just mixed in some pesticide with cat food and left them out in the garden. A cat will eat any-thing, you know." Hidaka put a cigarette in his mouth and lit it, taking a leisurely drag. The smoke dissipated in the breeze coming in through the window.

"But, why?" To tell the truth, I was a little disturbed by this revelation.

"I told you we haven't found a tenant yet?" His cold smile faded.

"Uh-huh."

"Our real estate agent's still looking, but when he was here the other day, he said something that bothered me."

"What's that?"

"He didn't think it made a good impression to have all those plastic bottles lined up in front of the house. It would make people think we had a problem with strays, which would make it hard to rent."

"So just throw away the bottles. They didn't work, anyway."

"Yeah, but that wouldn't solve the basic problem. What happens if someone comes here to check out the place and there's cat shit all over the garden? If we're here, we can clean it up, but what happens once we leave? I can't have the place smelling like a litter box."

"So you killed the cat?"

"Hey, the owner's as responsible for what happened as I am. Not that she seems to understand that at all." Hidaka stubbed out his cigarette in an ashtray.

"Does Rie know?"

The corner of his mouth curled up in another smile and he shook his head. "Are you kidding? Women love cats. If I told her the truth, she'd think I was the devil incarnate."

I sat in silence, at a loss for how to respond. Just then, the phone rang and Hidaka picked it up.

"Hello? . . . Oh, hi. I was wondering when you'd call. . . . Yes, all according to schedule. . . . Hey, okay, you got me. I was just about to start. . . . Sure, I should be able to get it done tonight. . . . Right, I'll send it along as soon as it's finished. . . . No, actually, this phone will be out of service after noon tomorrow. I'll have to call you. . . . Yes, from the hotel. Right, bye."

He hung up and gave a little sigh.

"Your editor?"

"Yes. My articles are usually late, but this time the stakes are a little bit higher. I mean, if he doesn't get it from me tonight, then he won't have it in time. I'll be out of the country by the day after tomorrow."

"Well." I stood from my chair. "I should probably get going then. I don't want to throw you off schedule."

The doorbell rang. "It's probably just a salesman," Hidaka said, but then we heard Rie walking down the hallway, followed by a knock at the office door.

"Yeah?" Hidaka called out.

She opened the door and peered in, a dark look on her face. "It's Ms. Fujio," she said quietly.

Hidaka's face clouded over like the sky before a squall. "Not her again."

"She says it's something she needs to talk to you about today."

"Great." Hidaka chewed his lip. "She must've found out we're moving to Canada."

"Should I say you're busy?"

"Yeah"—then, after a moment of thought—"no, I'll see her. Might as well get it over with now so I don't have to think about it later. You can let her up."

"If you're sure . . ." Rie glanced in my direction.

"Oh, don't worry about me," I said. "I was just leaving."

"Well, this is a fine pickle," Hidaka said with a sigh after she'd left the room.

"Is that Fujio as in Masaya Fujio?"

"Yeah, it's his sister. Her name's Miyako." Hidaka scratched his forehead beneath the longish locks of his hair. "If she just wanted some cash, that'd be easy enough. But a total recall? Rewrites? Give me a break."

More footsteps sounded in the hall. Hidaka's mouth snapped shut. I heard Rie apologizing for the lack of lights. A knock.

"Yes?" Hidaka said.

"Ms. Fujio," Rie said, opening the door.

Behind her stood a woman in her late twenties. She had long hair and was wearing the kind of suit that college grads wear to their first job interview. For an unexpected visitor, she had put a lot of attention into her presentation.

"So, I'll see you later," I said to Hidaka. I was about to tell him I'd come to see him off the day after tomorrow, but checked myself. I didn't know for sure if Ms. Fujio knew he was leaving and didn't want to rock any boats. Hidaka nodded quietly.

Rie walked me to the door. "Sorry to rush you out like this." She pressed her hands together apologetically, one eye closed in a wink. She was short and slender enough that the expression made her look like a young girl. It was hard to believe she was over thirty.

"That's okay. I'll come see you off the day after tomorrow."

"Oh, it's all right. We don't want to trouble you. I'm sure you're busy."

"No, it's no trouble at all. See you."

"Good-bye," she said, and stood watching me as I walked out the gate and turned the corner.

I was back at my apartment doing a bit of work when the doorbell rang. My place was a lot different from Hidaka's: a large studio apartment in a five-story building. The room was divided down the middle, with one side functioning as a combined workspace and bedroom, while the other, slightly larger side served as living room, dining room, and kitchen.

I didn't have a Rie of my own, so when the doorbell rang, there was no one to answer it but me.

I looked through the peephole, then opened the door. It was my editor, Oshima.

"Punctual as always," I said.

"It's the only thing I have going for me." He held out a nicely wrapped box from a famous Japanese sweet shop. "Here, a bribe."

He knows me too well.

"Sorry you had to come all the way out here."

He shook his head. "It was on my way home."

I motioned him in and poured some tea. Then I stepped into my office and brought out the manuscript that had been lying on the desk. "Can't say how good it is, but it's done. Here."

"Let me take a look."

He set down his cup and reached for the manuscript, beginning to read immediately. I opened a newspaper. It always made me uncomfortable to have people read my stuff in front of me.

He was about halfway through when the cordless phone on the dining-room table began to ring.

I got up and answered it. "Yes, Nonoguchi speaking."

"Hey, it's me." Hidaka's voice was somewhat muted.

"Hey there. What's up?" What I really wanted to know, though, was what had happened with Miyako Fujio.

He paused for a moment. "You busy?"

"Well, I've got someone here right now."

"Right. How long before you're free?"

I glanced at the clock on the wall. It was just after six. "Not long, I think. What's up?"

"Eh, it's not really a phone conversation. There's something I want to ask you about. Think you could come over?"

"Sure, no problem." I almost asked if this was about the Fujios, but I resisted. I'd almost forgotten Oshima was sitting right next to me.

"How about eight o'clock?"

"Sure thing."

"Great, I'll be waiting." He hung up.

I set down the phone and Oshima started to get up from the sofa.

"If you're busy, I can head out—"

"No, it's fine." I waved him back to his seat. "I made an appointment to meet a friend at eight. I've got plenty of time. Please, read."

"I see. Well then." He sat back and resumed reading.

I made another attempt to distract myself by reading the newspaper, but I couldn't stop thinking about Hidaka. He'd written a novel a couple of years earlier, *Forbidden Hunting Grounds*, which was about a woodblock artist. It was supposedly fiction but its main character was based on a real person: Masaya Fujio.

Fujio had gone to the same middle school as Hidaka and me, and a lot of what the three of us had done and seen together ended up in the book. This would have been fine, especially since he changed everyone's name, but the novel revealed some things that Masaya Fujio wouldn't have been particularly proud to see in print. All of the various misadventures of his student life were detailed pretty much as they'd happened in real life, including the shocking finale, where Masaya is stabbed to death by a prostitute.

The book became a bestseller. Anyone who'd known Masaya could easily guess who the model for the novel's main character had been. Of course, someone in the Fujio family eventually saw it.

Masaya's father had already passed away, but his mother and sister raised a fuss. They said it was obvious that Masaya was the model for the book and that they had never granted permission to Hidaka to write such a book about him. The book was a violation of their family's privacy, and a stain on Masaya's reputation. They demanded that all copies of the novel be pulled from the shelves, and that the novel be extensively rewritten before it was republished.

As Hidaka had said, it didn't seem to be about money. Though there was still some doubt as to whether the demand for rewrites was sincere, or simply a negotiation tactic.

Judging from his voice on the phone, the negotiations hadn't gone well. Still, I wondered why he'd called me. Maybe he was really in a fix. Maybe things had somehow gotten worse. I wondered how I could help.

As I sat there lost in thought, Oshima finished reading the manuscript. "Seems good to me. Laid-back, a bit nostalgic. I like it."

"That's good to hear." I was genuinely relieved. I took a long sip of my tea. Oshima was a good kid, not the type to offer empty praise.

Normally, we would then have discussed what was to come next, but I had agreed to go see Hidaka soon. I looked at the clock. Six thirty.

"You good on time?" Oshima asked.

"I'm fine, but I was thinking—there's a decent restaurant near here. Why don't we eat while we talk?"

"Sure thing. I have to eat, too, after all." Oshima put the manuscript in his bag. If I remembered correctly, he was almost thirty, but still single.

The restaurant, one of those family places, was only a two- or three-minute walk from my apartment. We talked over casserole and mostly we just chatted about this and that. But I brought up the subject of Hidaka.

When I did, Oshima looked surprised. "You know him?"

"We went to the same elementary school and middle school. We grew up right around the corner from each other and not far from here. You could walk to our old neighborhood from here, though, of course, neither of our houses are still there. They were torn down to build apartment buildings years ago."

"So, you were childhood friends."

"We keep in touch."

"Wow." Oshima was obviously impressed. I could see the envious longing in his eyes. "I had no idea."

"Actually, he was the one who brought my work to your magazine."

"You don't say."

"Yeah, your editorial director asked Hidaka to submit a piece but he turned them down, saying he didn't do children's fiction. Instead, he brought me in to meet with the editor in chief. You could say I owe him one." I lifted a forkful of macaroni to my mouth.

"Huh! I hadn't heard that. It'd be interesting to see what Hidaka would do with children's literature, though." Oshima looked up at me. "What about you, Mr. Nonoguchi? Have you ever thought of writing something for adults?"

"Someday, maybe. If the opportunity presents itself." I meant it.

We left the restaurant at seven thirty and walked to the station together. We were going in different directions, so I said good-bye to Oshima at the platform. My train came soon after that.

I reached Hidaka's at exactly eight o'clock. I first noticed something was wrong when I got to the front door. The house was completely dark, and even the entranceway light was off.

I tried the intercom button anyway, but there was no reply.

At first, I thought I'd misunderstood him. Hidaka had definitely asked me to come at eight, but maybe he hadn't meant for us to meet at his house.

When there was no answer at the front door, I left and

started walking back toward the station. Along the way was a small park with a pay phone by its entrance. I pulled out my wallet and stepped into the booth.

I got the number for the Crown Hotel from information and then called and asked for Hidaka. The desk put me through immediately and Rie answered, "Hello?"

"It's me, Nonoguchi. Is Hidaka in?"

"No, he hasn't come to the hotel yet. I think he's still at home. He still had some work left to do."

"I don't think he's there." I explained that I'd been to the house and it didn't look like anyone was home.

"He said he wouldn't be here until pretty late."

"So maybe he just went out for a bit then?"

"That doesn't sound right, either." Rie went quiet. "Look, how about I come and take a look," she said after a minute. "I should be there in about forty minutes. Where are you now?"

I told her that I could kill time at the local café and then meet her at the house when she got there. After hanging up, I left the phone booth, but before going to the café I decided to take one more look at Hidaka's place. When I got there, the lights were still all out. But this time, I noticed that the Saab was parked in the driveway. That bothered me.

The café was a specialty coffee shop and one of Hidaka's favorite places to go when he wanted a change of scenery. I'd been there several times, and the owner recognized me and asked after Hidaka. I told him I was supposed to meet up with Hidaka, but that he'd been a no-show. We talked about baseball for a good half hour before I paid my tab and left, walking quickly back toward the Hidaka residence.

I got to the front gate just as Rie was getting out of a taxi.

I called out to her and she smiled at me. But when she looked at the house, her face clouded over. "There really isn't a single light on."

"I guess he's still out."

"But he didn't say he'd be going anywhere."

She walked to the front door, pulling the keys out of her bag. I followed along behind her. The door was locked. She unlocked it, went inside, and started turning on lights. It was cool inside the house. Empty.

Rie walked down the hallway to Hidaka's office. This door was also locked.

"Does he always lock the office door before leaving?" I asked.

She shook her head as she fished another key from her purse. "Not much recently."

She opened the door. The lights in the office were off, but it wasn't completely dark. The computer was on, and a pale glow came from the monitor. Rie felt along the wall for the light switch, then she abruptly stopped.

Hidaka was lying in the middle of the room, his feet pointing toward the door.

After being frozen for a few seconds, Rie dashed over to him. But before she reached him, she stopped in her tracks, frozen again, her hands pressed to her mouth.

Gingerly, I approached. Hidaka was lying facedown with his head twisted so I could see the left side of his face. His eyes were half-open. They were the eyes of a corpse.

"He's dead," I said.

Rie slowly collapsed to the floor. The sobs came welling up the moment her knees touched the carpet.

. . .

While the police were examining the scene, Rie and I waited in the living room. At least, it used to be the living room; now that both the sofa and the table were gone, it felt a little bare. Rie sat on a cardboard box filled with magazines, while I paced in circles like a bear, occasionally poking my head out into the hallway to see how the investigation was proceeding. Rie was crying the whole time. I looked at my wristwatch: 10:30 p.m.

Finally, there was a knock and the door opened. Detective Sakoda came in—a calm fellow, approaching fifty. He seemed to be in charge of the investigation.

"Might I have a few words?" he asked me after glancing at Rie.

"Sure, anything."

"I'm fine to talk, too." Rie dabbed at her eyes with a handkerchief. Tears were still in her voice, but her words were clear. I remembered what Hidaka had said earlier that day, about her being able to dig in when it mattered.

"It won't take long."

Detective Sakoda asked us to tell him everything that had happened that day up until we found the body. I started first, and as I talked, I realized my story would have to include Miyako Fujio.

"Around what time did Hidaka call?" Detective Sakoda asked.

"It was a little after six, I think."

"And did he mention Ms. Fujio when you spoke?"

"No, he just said he wanted to talk to me about something."

"So it could've been about something else?"

"It's possible."

"Any idea what that might have been?"

"No, not at all."

The detective nodded, then turned to Rie. "Around what time did Ms. Fujio go home?"

"After five, I think."

"And did you speak with your husband after that?"

"A little."

"How did he seem?"

"Upset. The talk with Ms. Fujio hadn't gone so well. But he told me it was nothing to worry about."

"And it was after that when you left the house and went to the hotel?"

"That's right."

The detective nodded. "Okay, so you were planning to stay at the Crown Hotel tonight and tomorrow night, then leave for Canada the day after tomorrow? But your husband had some work to finish, so he stayed behind at the house." Sakoda looked over his notes as he spoke, then looked back up at Rie. "Who knew that your husband would be at home alone?"

"Well, myself and . . ." She looked at me.

"Of course I knew. And I expect that someone at the magazine, *Somei Monthly,* would have known as well." I explained that Hidaka had been writing a serialized novel for them and it was the next installment that he was staying behind to finish. "Still, that hardly narrows down your suspects."

"I'm just collecting facts," Detective Sakoda said, smiling ever so slightly.

He then asked Rie whether she'd seen any suspicious people around their house lately. She said no. That was when

I remembered the woman I'd seen in the garden earlier that day. I wondered if I should say something, but ultimately kept silent. Who would commit murder to avenge a cat?

When the questions were done, the detective said he would have one of his men take me home. I would've preferred to stay with Rie, but it sounded as if they had already called her parents and someone was coming to pick her up.

As the shock of discovering Hidaka's body gradually faded, I could feel a wave of exhaustion coming over me. I felt bleak inside when I thought of walking all the way to the station and taking the train all the way home. I decided to accept the offer of a ride home from the police.

A crowd of police were still outside the room, mostly walking back and forth down the hall. The door to the office was open, but I couldn't see inside and I assumed the body had already been removed.

A uniformed officer called out to me and led me to a police car parked outside the front gate. It was the closest I'd been to a police vehicle since the time I was pulled over for speeding. A tall man was standing next to the cruiser. If he was a police officer, he was in plainclothes, but the way the streetlights fell on him made it hard to see his face.

"Long time no see, Mr. Nonoguchi," he said.

"Do I know you?" I stopped, squinting at the man's face.

He stepped forward out of the shadows. It was a familiar face, with narrow eyebrows and close-set eyes. I knew I knew him, but it took a moment for the memory to surface.

"Do you remember me?"

"I do! Er . . ." I thought for a moment. "Kaga, right?"

"In the flesh." He bowed politely. "It's been a while."

"It certainly has." I nodded back to him. I looked at him again. He had good features, and age had improved them. It had been at least a decade since I'd seen him, maybe longer. "I'd heard you'd joined the police force. Never imagined our reunion would be under these circumstances."

"I was surprised, too. When I heard who discovered the body, I wondered if it was someone else with the same name. At least until I saw your business card."

"Nonoguchi isn't the most common surname out there, I know." I shook my head. "What a coincidence!"

"We can talk in the car. I'll give you a lift. Sorry it's not a private car." He opened the rear door for me. The uniformed officer got into the driver's seat.

Kaga, fresh out of graduate school, had come to work at the middle school where I used to teach social studies. Like most new teachers, he was passionate about the job. An accomplished kendo practitioner, he'd taken over the school's kendo club, and he made quite an impression on the other teachers.

He'd quit teaching after only two years for a number of reasons, though as far as I could tell, none of it was his fault. Still, I suspect he wasn't cut out to be a teacher in the first place. However, I'm sure his departure from the school had more to do with the way things were going for him at the time.

"Which school are you at now?" Kaga asked, soon after the car started down the street.

Kaga. That's what I'd called him when he was a new hire at the school. I'd have to remember to call him *Detective* Kaga now.

I shook my head. "I was working at a middle school in my hometown until just a little while ago. I quit back in March."

Kaga look surprised. "You don't say? What are you doing now?"

"Well, it's not glamorous, but I'm a writer. I write stories for children."

"No kidding! Is that how you knew Kunihiko Hidaka?"

"Not exactly." I explained our past. Kaga nodded with every detail. I wondered if Detective Sakoda hadn't told him anything, since I'd certainly included this in my earlier statement.

"So you started writing while you were still teaching?"

"That's right. But not much. Just a couple of short stories a year. When I finally made up my mind to try my hand at being a real writer, I realized I had to quit my job."

"I see. That's quite a decision." Kaga sounded impressed. I wondered if he was comparing my choice to his own. Of course, even he had to realize there was a big difference between switching professions in your early twenties and doing it when you're much older, with four decades already under your belt.

"What sort of novels did Mr. Hidaka write?"

I looked at him. "You mean you haven't heard of Kunihiko Hidaka?"

"Sorry. I'd heard the name, but I've never read any of his books. I don't read many books these days."

"I'm sure you're busy."

"No, just lazy. I know I should read more, two or three a month." He put a hand to his head. *Two or three books a month* had been my catchphrase back when I was teaching composition. If Kaga had been making an intentional reference, it was a good one.

I gave him the digest version of Hidaka's career, starting

with his debut ten years ago. Then there were the awards and his rise to the bestseller lists. I also mentioned that he wrote works of pure literature as well as pure entertainment.

"Did he write anything I might be interested in?" Kaga asked. "Like murder mysteries?"

"Only a few, but yeah."

"Tell me the titles so I can look them up."

I mentioned Hidaka's novel *Sea Ghost*. I'd read it a long time ago and didn't remember it all that well, but it was definitely about a murder.

"Do you know why Hidaka wanted to move to Canada?" Kaga asked when I was finished.

"I think he had a few reasons, but mostly, I think he was just tired. He'd been talking about going overseas and taking it easy for several years now. The decision to move to Vancouver was Rie's."

"Rie is the wife, yes? She seemed young."

"They just got married last month. It was his second marriage."

"And his first wife, are they divorced?"

"No, she died in a car accident. That was five years ago already."

The realization that Hidaka was no longer in this world hit me again, hard. I wondered what he'd wanted to talk to me about this evening. I wondered if I had just ended my unimportant meeting and gone to see him right away, I might have saved him. I knew there was no point in thinking about it, yet the regret was hard to keep down.

"I heard there was some trouble with a Mr. Fujio, someone he'd used as the subject of one of his novels?" Kaga said.

"Can you think of any other troubles he might have had? Anything from his novels or personal life?"

"Nothing I can think of." I realized for the first time that this was an interrogation. Suddenly, the complete silence from the police officer driving the car made me uncomfortable.

"By the way," Kaga said, opening his notebook, "do you know anyone by the name of Namiko Nishizaki?"

"What?"

"I have two other names, too: Tetsuji Osano and Hajime Nakane."

"Oh, right," I said, finally understanding. "Those are characters in *The Gates of Ice*, the serialized novel that Hidaka's writing." I wondered what would happen to the serial now. I supposed they'd have to abandon it midstory.

"It seems he was working on it right up until the moment of his death."

"Ah! His computer was left on, wasn't it?"

"The document he was writing was open."

"I see." Something occurred to me. "How much of the novel had he written?"

"What do you mean by how much?"

"How many pages?"

I explained that Hidaka had told me he had to write thirty pages that night.

"It was more than a couple of pages," Detective Kaga said.

"I wonder if you could nail down the time of death by the number of pages he'd written. You see, he hadn't even started working on it when I left the house."

"Yes, we considered that. But as you well know, writing is

a start-and-stop kind of thing. It's hard to estimate the time based on his progress."

"That's true, but you could at least figure out what his maximum speed was, and then come up with a shortest-possible time estimate."

"Interesting," Kaga said. "What do you think Hidaka's maximum speed was, then?"

"Good question. He told me once that he averaged four pages an hour."

"So even if he was rushing, you'd say a reasonable top limit might be about six pages?"

"That sounds about right."

Detective Kaga fell silent. He seemed to be doing some calculations in his head.

"What is it?"

"It's hard to say." Kaga shook his head. "I'm not even sure if the document he had up on the screen was the part of the serial he was working on."

"You mean he might've been looking at an earlier part of the novel."

"Yes. We're going to visit the publisher tomorrow to try to find that out."

I quickly turned the situation over in my mind. According to Rie, Miyako Fujio had gone home around five o'clock. It was after six when the phone call from Hidaka came. If he'd been writing during the time that we knew he was alive, he could've written five or six pages, max. That meant the question was, how many more pages had he actually written?

"I understand you might not be able to disclose this," I said to Detective Kaga, "but do you have an estimated time of death?"

"You're right, I can't disclose that, or at least, I shouldn't." Kaga chuckled. "But I suppose it doesn't really matter. We're still waiting on an autopsy for the final results, but we're pretty sure it happened sometime between five and seven o'clock."

"Except, he called me after six."

"True. Which would make the time of death somewhere between six and seven o'clock."

Wait.

That meant that he'd been killed right after he talked to me on the phone.

"How was he killed?" I said, half to myself. Kaga gave me a wondering look. He must've thought that was a strange question for the one who discovered the body. But it was true, I didn't remember seeing anything that would tell me how he'd died. To be honest, I was frightened. I don't think I even looked that closely at him.

I explained myself and Kaga nodded, understanding. "That's also something we need to wait on the autopsy to be sure, but all indications are that he was strangled."

"You mean someone choked him? Like, with their hands, or a rope?"

"A telephone cord. It was still wrapped around his neck."

"What?" I had no recollection of seeing the telephone.

"He had one other injury, besides. It appears he was struck in the back of the head. We believe the weapon was a brass paperweight. We found it on the floor next to him."

"So someone hit him on the back of the head, knocked him out, then strangled him?"

"That's the most likely explanation." Detective Kaga lowered his voice. "I'm sure there will be an announcement soon, but please don't repeat any of this before that, okay?"

"Sure, of course."

The car finally arrived at my apartment.

"Thanks for the ride. That was much better than having to take the train."

"Not at all. Thanks for the chat. It was very helpful."

As I started getting out of the car, Kaga stopped me. "Tell me the name of the magazine."

"His serial is being published in *Somei Monthly*."

Kaga shook his head. "No. I meant the magazine you're writing for, Mr. Nonoguchi."

I grinned sheepishly and blurted out the name. Kaga wrote it down in his notes and we said our good-nights.

Back in my apartment, I sat vacantly on the sofa for a while. I tried thinking back over the events of the day, but none of it felt real. It was the kind of day you seldom experience, if ever. The thought came to me that, even though it had been tragic, it was almost a shame to have such a day end by merely going to sleep. Not that I would be able to sleep, anyway. Not tonight.

Then I had an idea. I should record my experience. I should write the story of how my friend was killed.

That is the story behind these notes. I've decided I will keep writing them until the case is solved and the truth is out.

Hidaka's death was in the morning paper. I hadn't watched TV the night before, but I guessed the story was probably out by the eleven o'clock news.

The newspaper had a simple headline on the side of the front page, with the article continued on the interior. There was a big picture of Hidaka's house and, right next to it, a publicity shot of him that was probably taken for some magazine.

The article laid out the facts more or less accurately with one notable exception. Concerning the discovery of the body, it read, "Hearing from an acquaintance that the lights in the house were out, his wife, Rie, returned home to find Hidaka dead in the first-floor office," which might make people think that Rie was the only one there. My name wasn't mentioned anywhere.

According to the article, the investigators were looking into two possibilities. One was that Hidaka's death was premeditated murder, and the other that it was incidental manslaughter. The front door had been locked, so the journalist assumed the criminal got in through the office window.

I closed the paper and was about to start making breakfast when the doorbell rang. I looked at the clock and it was just after eight. It was unusually early for callers. I almost never use my door intercom, I simply go and open the door, but today, I picked it up.

"Yes?"

"Mr. Nonoguchi?" The voice was of a woman, breathing hard, as if she had been running.

"Yes, who is this?"

"Sorry to drop by so early. I'm from Channel Eight News and I was hoping we could talk to you about what happened last night."

That was a surprise. My name wasn't in the papers, but the TV newspeople had clearly caught wind that someone else was present when the body was discovered.

"Erm . . ." I considered my response. I didn't want to say anything lightly that might come back to haunt me. "What exactly is this about?"

"The author Kunihiko Hidaka was murdered in his home last night. We heard that you were there with his wife when the body was found. Is this true? Mr. Nonoguchi?"

Channel 8 News was one of those variety news shows. Her tone was overly deferential, almost sycophantic. I rolled my eyes. Still, it wouldn't do to lie.

"Yes, that's true."

Even over the intercom, I could feel the excitement on the other side.

"And why were you visiting Mr. Hidaka's house that night?"

"Sorry, I can't discuss this with you. I've told everything to the police."

"We heard that you contacted the wife, Rie, after seeing something strange about the house. Can you comment on what you thought was strange?"

"Please, talk to the police." I hung up the intercom.

I had heard that TV news crews could be extremely rude, but this was my first time experiencing it for myself. Why couldn't they understand that I didn't want to talk to anyone so soon after finding my friend dead?

I decided I wouldn't go outside and risk running into another TV crew. I felt that I should pay Rie a visit or maybe just check on the house, but it would be impossible to get near the place today.

I was warming up a mug of milk in the microwave when the doorbell rang again. Again I picked up the intercom.

"Hi, this is Channel Four News. I was hoping I could talk to you?" This time it was a man's voice. "Mr. Nonoguchi, every person in the country is waiting to hear more details about what happened."

This kind of bombastic statement would, under other circumstances, have made me chuckle.

"Look, all I did was find him. I don't know anything else."

"But you were friends with Mr. Hidaka, correct?"

"That's true, but I can't talk to you about anything that happened last night."

"If you could come out and tell us anything about Mr. Hidaka, that would be fine." The man was persistent.

I sighed. I was worried less about the imposition and more about the trouble it would cause my neighbors if news crews were camped outside my door all day.

I hung up the receiver, went to my door, and opened it. A forest of microphones were thrust into my face.

In the end, my entire morning was spent fielding interviews, and I didn't even get to eat a proper breakfast. Finally, a little after noon, I retreated back inside my apartment. I was eating some instant udon noodles and watching TV when I saw a close-up of my face on the screen. I choked on my noodles. I couldn't believe they were already playing the footage they had taken just a couple of hours before.

"You were friends from elementary school, correct? What sort of person would you say Mr. Hidaka was?" the female reporter asked in a shrill voice.

On the screen, I seem to be thinking far too deeply about the question. I had noticed at the time that my silence was uncomfortably long. I guessed they hadn't had the time to edit out this awkward pause in the footage. You could see the reporters around me growing impatient.

"He had a strong personality," the me on the screen said at last. "He was a real individual. Sometimes you'd think he was the most amazing guy, then other times you'd be surprised by his coldness. But perhaps you can say that about anyone."

"Can you give an example of what you mean by his coldness?"

"Well . . ." Then the me on the screen shook his head. "No, not off the top of my head. And this really isn't the time or the place."

Of course, in my head I was picturing Hidaka killing that cat, but it wasn't the kind of thing to announce on the public airwaves.

After a series of increasingly inappropriate questions, the female reporter asked, "Is there anything you want to say to Hidaka's killer?"

This was it, her home-run question.

"Not at this time," I answered. You could tell she was disappointed.

After that, they cut back to the studio, where a reporter talked about Hidaka's novels. Behind the many varied worlds he had created, the reporter said, were the complicated human relations of the author himself. This clearly suggested that his death might be related to the intersection of his literary and private lives.

The reporter talked about the recent troubles Hidaka had had with his novel *Forbidden Hunting Grounds*. How the family of the man who was the model for the book's main character had raised objections. Apparently word hadn't yet got out that Miyako Fujio had been to Hidaka's house the day he died.

Then they went to a panel of celebrity guests they'd brought into the studio, and they started talking about Hidaka's death. I got a sour taste in my mouth and turned off the television.

I wished the NHK would cover the situation. For accurate information about something big, one of their networks was usually the best option. Unfortunately, the death of Hidaka wasn't momentous enough for a publicly funded station to put together a special program.

The phone rang. I'd lost count how many times it had already rung that day, but I still picked up on the off chance it might be something to do with work.

"Yes, Nonoguchi speaking," I said a little roughly.

"Hi, it's me." The firm voice on the other side was without a doubt Rie.

"Oh, hi. How did you do last night?" It was a strange question, but I couldn't think of anything else to ask.

"I went to stay at my parents' house. I thought I should probably call people, tell them what happened, but I just didn't have it in me."

"I can imagine. Where are you now?"

"Home. I got a call from the police this morning, and they said they wanted to go over the scene with me and ask me a few more questions."

"Has that happened already?"

"Yes. Though some of the detectives are still around."

"What about the media? They giving you any trouble?"

"Of course. But some of the people from Hidaka's publisher and some television people that knew him came over, and they're handling the questions. It's taken a load off my shoulders."

"I see." I was going to say that was good, but swallowed my words. It didn't seem like the right thing to say to a woman who'd lost her husband the night before.

"How about you, Mr. Nonoguchi? They must be pestering you endlessly. I didn't see it myself, but one of the people from the publisher said you were on TV. I was worried so I called."

"Oh, don't worry about me. I think they've finally settled down."

"I'm really sorry you had to go through this." I could hear her apology was sincere, and I was impressed with her mental fortitude. By all rights, she should have been one of the saddest people in the world right then, but she was taking the time to worry about me. *She really does have spine,* I thought again.

"Please let me know if there's anything I can help with. Anything at all," I told her.

"I think I'm okay. Some of my husband's relatives are here, and my mother, too."

"Okay." I remembered that Hidaka had a brother two years older than him, and that the brother and his wife had taken in his mother. "Well, if there's anything, don't hesitate to ask."

"Thank you so much. I'll talk to you later."

"Thanks for calling."

I hung up, but my thoughts remained on Rie. I wondered what she would do now, how she would live. She was still young, and I'd heard that her family was well-off, with money from the freight business, so she probably wouldn't struggle. However, I figured it would probably take quite some time for her to recover from the shock. After all, they'd only been married a month.

Before meeting Hidaka, Rie had been a passionate fan of his novels. They'd met through her work and had started dating soon after. That meant that last night she lost two important things: one was her husband, the other was the author Kunihiko Hidaka's new novel.

I was still lost in thought when the phone rang again. They wanted me to appear on a variety news program. I turned them down on the spot.

Detective Kaga arrived a little after six that evening. I answered the doorbell with a despondent certainty that it was the press again and found him on my doorstep instead. He wasn't alone. He'd brought another, slightly younger detective with him, named Makimura.

"Sorry to bother you. I had two or three more questions."

"I expected as much. Come on in."

Detective Kaga didn't even move to take off his shoes but asked, "Were you in the middle of dinner?"

"No, I haven't eaten yet. I was thinking of getting something, though."

"How about we eat out? To tell the truth, we've been so busy conducting interviews that we didn't have time for a proper lunch. Did we?" He looked to his partner, and Detective Makimura obliged with a sheepish smile.

"Okay, sure. Where would you like to go? There's a pretty good pork-cutlet place near here."

"We're fine anywhere." Then Kaga hesitated as though he'd just thought of something. "There was a family restaurant just down the street, right? The one you went to with Mr. Oshima, your editor."

"That's right. Do you want to go there?"

"Actually, yes. It's close, and they have free coffee refills."

"I can get behind that," Detective Makimura chimed in.

"It's fine by me," I said. "Let me get my jacket."

I went to get changed, leaving them at the door. I wondered why Kaga wanted to go to that restaurant. Did he have some reason for wanting to see it? Or was it just because it was close and he could drink coffee?

I hadn't come to any conclusions by the time I joined them in the hallway.

At the restaurant, I ordered shrimp Doria. Detective Kaga and Detective Makimura ordered lamb steak and meat loaf respectively.

"So, about that novel," Kaga said once the waitress had left. "The one that was left open on Mr. Hidaka's computer screen? *The Gates of Ice,* was it?"

"Right. You were wondering whether the open file was something he'd written yesterday or something already published that he was looking over, right? Did you figure it out?"

"We did. It looks like it was new material, written yesterday. We talked to the editor at *Somei Monthly,* and he said it fit perfectly together with what had been written before."

"So he was working hard until he was killed."

"There was something odd, though." Detective Kaga leaned slightly forward and rested his right elbow on the table.

"Something odd?"

"The number of pages. We worked out how many pages the file would be when printed out, and it came out to twenty-seven-odd pages. Even if he had started writing immediately after Miss Fujio went home at five o'clock, that seems like too many. Based on what you told us yesterday, he could only write four to six pages in an hour."

"Twenty-seven pages? That is quite a lot."

I went back to Hidaka's house at eight o'clock, but even if he'd been alive and working right up to the moment I arrived, he'd have to have written nine pages an hour.

"So," I said, "maybe he was lying?"

"What do you mean?"

"Maybe he'd already written ten or twelve pages when I saw him before. Maybe he just wanted to act like he hadn't started yet—you know, maintaining appearances and all that."

"That's what the editor at the publisher suggested, too."

"Thought so." I nodded.

"But Hidaka had told Rie when she left the house that he wouldn't make it to the hotel until rather late. Despite that, by eight o'clock, he already had twenty-seven pages written. Since each installment of *The Gates of Ice* was around thirty pages, he was almost finished. I understand writers are often late, but do they ever finish early?"

"I suppose. Writing isn't a purely mechanical operation. You can spend hours at your desk without writing a single page. But when inspiration strikes, sometimes it's hard to stop writing."

"Was Mr. Hidaka that kind of writer?"

"He was. Which is to say, I think most authors are that kind of writer."

"I see. I wouldn't know anything about that." Detective Kaga settled back into his seat.

"I'm not sure why you're so hung up on the number of pages he'd finished before he was killed," I said. "The basic facts are, when Rie left the house, his story wasn't finished, but when the body was found, it was almost finished. All that means is that he did some amount of work in the time before he was killed. Right?"

"Maybe so." Detective Kaga nodded, but he still looked unsatisfied.

Kaga, my former colleague, now a detective, seemed unable to let even the slightest detail go without thoroughly working it over. I suppose that was part of the job.

The waitress brought our food and talk ceased for a while.

"By the way," I asked eventually, "what happened with the remains? You mentioned there was going to be an autopsy?"

"Yes, they did it today." Detective Kaga looked over at Makimura. "You were there, right?"

"No, not me. If I was, I wouldn't be eating this now." He frowned as he stabbed his meat loaf with a fork.

"True enough." Kaga smiled wryly. He turned back to me. "What about the autopsy?"

"I was just wondering if they had determined a time of death."

"I haven't read the reports myself, but I heard they had a pretty good estimate."

"Are they sure it's accurate?"

"It depends on what they based the estimate on. For example—" Kaga began, but then he shook his head. "No, I should save that for later."

"Why?"

"I don't want to ruin your shrimp Doria," he said, indicating my plate.

"Indeed." I nodded. "Let's let that one rest for now, then."

Detective Kaga nodded to indicate I'd made a wise choice.

While we ate, he said nothing about the case. Instead, he asked about the children's books I was writing. He wanted to know what the current trends were. What were people reading? What did I think about the decline in reading overall?

I told him that the books aimed at children and teens that were selling were the ones that the Ministry of Education had promoted as "library recommendations," and that the decline in reading among children was largely the fault of their parents.

"Parents these days don't read books themselves, but they feel they should make their children read. Since they aren't readers, however, they have no idea what to give their children. That's why they cling to the recommendations from the Ministry of Education. Those books are all insufferably boring, and as a result, the kids learn to hate books. It's a vicious cycle, with no end in sight."

Both of the detectives listened to my story with the appearance of rapt attention while they ate. I secretly wondered whether they had the slightest interest at all.

Coffee came after the meal. I ordered myself a hot milk.

"You smoke, right?" Detective Kaga said, gesturing toward an ashtray.

"No, no thanks," I said.

"What, you quit?"

"Yeah, about two years ago. Doctor's orders. It was wrecking my stomach."

"I see. Sorry, we should have sat in the nonsmoking section. I guess when I think of authors, I always imagine them smoking. Mr. Hidaka was a pretty heavy smoker, too, wasn't he?"

"That's right. Sometimes I thought he was fumigating his office to keep the bugs out."

"How about last night when you found the body? Was there still smoke in the room?"

"I wonder . . . I was a little upset, as you can imagine." I took a sip of my milk. "Now that you mention it, I think there was a little smoke."

"I see." Detective Kaga brought his cup to his lips. Setting it down, he slowly pulled out his notebook. "Actually, there was one other thing I wanted to check with you. About when you went to Hidaka's house at eight o'clock?"

"Yes?"

"You said that since no one answered the intercom, and all the lights in the house were off, you called the hotel where Rie was staying, correct?"

"That's right."

"So, about those lights." Detective Kaga looked straight at me. "Are you sure they were all off? All of them?"

"They were off, without a doubt." I stared right back.

"But you can't see the office window from the gate, can you? Did you go around to the back garden?"

"No, I didn't. But you can tell from the gate whether the lights are on in the office or not."

"Really? How's that?" Detective Kaga asked.

"There's a large cherry tree right in front of his office window. If the office lights are on, you can see it clearly."

Detectives Kaga and Makimura nodded. "That makes sense."

"Was that a big problem?"

"No, we're just dotting our i's here. If we don't get every detail in the report, our boss gets mad at us."

"Sounds tough."

"It's like any other job." Kaga smiled in a way that reminded me of when he'd been a teacher.

"So how is the investigation going? Have you made any progress?" I looked at each of the detectives in turn, before settling on Detective Kaga.

"Well, we're really just getting started," he said softly, as if trying to suggest they weren't supposed to talk about it.

"On the news," I said, "they were saying it might have been a happenstance murder. That someone might have just broken in, found him there, and had to kill him."

"Well, it's not entirely out of the question," Detective Kaga said.

"By which you mean it's out of the question."

"Pretty much." Detective Kaga had one eye on his partner. "Personally, I feel it's highly unlikely."

"Why's that?"

"Well, typically, someone breaking and entering with intent to steal will go in through the front door. That way, if they're discovered, they might be able to talk their way out of it. They also tend to leave via the front door. But as you know, the front door to Mr. Hidaka's house was locked."

"And thieves don't generally lock up behind themselves?"

"The dead bolt on the front door can only be locked from the inside when it's closed, or from the outside with a key. The Hidaka house had three keys, and Rie had two of them. The third one was in Mr. Hidaka's trouser pocket."

"But some robbers still come in through the window, don't they?"

"That's true, but they tend to be the ones who've done the most prior planning. They case the place first, learning when the residents are out, making sure they can't be seen from the street, and so on, before they act."

"And nothing suggests that might've happened?"

"Well"—Detective Kaga smiled, showing white teeth—"if anyone had cased the place, they'd have realized there was very little left in that house worth stealing."

My mouth opened in a perfect O. Detective Makimura was smiling slightly.

"Personally . . . ," Detective Kaga began, then stopped as though hesitant to say more. He started over. "I think it was someone who knew him."

"Well, that's troubling."

"Just between you and me." He raised a single finger to his lips.

"Of course." I nodded.

He glanced at Detective Makimura. The junior detective then picked up the check, stood up, and headed over to the cash register.

"Oh, no, I'll get it."

"No need." Detective Kaga held out a hand to stop me. "We were the ones who invited you out after all."

"But they don't pay for your meals, do they?"

"No, not for dinner, unfortunately."

"Sorry about that."

"No worries."

"Still." I looked over at the cash register. Detective Makimura was paying.

Something about what he was doing was strange. He was talking to the woman at the cash register. She glanced over in my direction, then turned back to Makimura and said something.

"Sorry," Detective Kaga said without even glancing toward the cash register. He was staring directly at me and his expression hadn't changed. "We're just checking your alibi."

"My alibi?"

"Yeah." He nodded. "We already checked with Mr. Oshima, your editor at Dojisha Publishing. But we have to corroborate as many details as we can. That's just how we do things. I hope you understand."

"Is that why you wanted to come here?"

"If we didn't come at the same time of day, there might be a different person working the register on that shift."

"I see," I said, deeply impressed.

Detective Makimura returned. Kaga nodded to him. "They overcharge us for anything?"

"Not a thing."

"That's good for a change," Kaga said, looking toward me, his eyes narrowing in the suggestion of a smile.

When I told him I was keeping a record of the last couple of days, Detective Kaga was interested in seeing it. We'd already left the restaurant and were walking back toward my apartment. If I hadn't said anything, we would probably have parted ways there.

"I figured I wouldn't have another experience like this in my life, so I should probably write it down. I think it's just part of being an author."

The detective thought about that for a while, then said, "I wonder if you'd let me read your account?"

"Read it? You? I don't know. I never wrote it with the intention of having someone read it. . . ."

"Please." He bowed his head to me. Next to him, Detective Makimura did the same.

"Enough of that. What will people think when they see two policemen bowing to me by the side of the road? Besides, I've already told you everything."

"I'd still like to see it."

"Well, if you insist." I scratched my head. "Can you come up to the apartment? I have it all in a file on my word processor, so you'll have to wait while I print it out."

"Not a problem," Kaga said.

The two detectives accompanied me up to my apartment. As I was printing out the manuscript, Detective Kaga came and looked over my shoulder. "You use a word processor?"

"I do."

"I noticed that Mr. Hidaka was using a regular computer."

"Well, he uses it for other things besides writing. E-mail, games, all kinds of things."

"You don't use a computer, Mr. Nonoguchi?"

"A word processor's enough for me."

"And how do you deliver your manuscripts to the publisher? Do they come and pick them up?"

"No, usually I send them by fax. Right over there." I pointed to the fax machine sitting in the corner of my room. I only had one phone line so my cordless phone was attached to the fax.

"But your editor did come over yesterday to pick up your manuscript." Kaga looked up. Maybe it was just my imagination, but I thought I saw a keen gleam in his eyes. I remembered what Detective Kaga said about Hidaka's killer having known him.

"There were a bunch of things we needed to talk about in person, so I asked him to make a special trip out to see me yesterday."

Kaga listened to my response in silence, nodding, but said nothing more.

When the printout was finished, I handed it to him, saying, "Actually, there was one thing I haven't told you yet."

"Really?" Detective Kaga didn't look particularly surprised.

"You'll see once you've read this. I didn't think it had anything to do with the case, and I didn't want to cast suspicion on a stranger."

What I was talking about, of course, was Hidaka and the cat.

"I understand. I know that happens." Detective Kaga thanked me profusely, and the two detectives headed out.

Well now.

I began writing today's entry right after Kaga and his companion left. The continuation of what I handed to them, that is. I know he might want to read this, too, but I will try not to dwell on that as I write. Otherwise, what's the point?

· · ·

Two days have passed since Hidaka's murder. The funeral took place at a Buddhist temple several kilometers from the house. A throng of publishing-industry people were in attendance, and the line to offer incense was long.

The TV crews were there as well. While the reporters were wearing their serious faces, they were, like snakes hunting, looking around for any dramatic scenes. If any of the mourners even looked as if they might be in danger of tearing up, the cameras would be on them in a flash.

After I had offered my incense, I stood by the reception tent, watching the mourners as they arrived. There were a few celebrities. I recognized some actors who had played some of Hidaka's characters in the movies made from his novels.

A reading of scriptures and a brief talk by the head priest followed the offering of incense. Rie was wearing a black suit, prayer beads clutched in her hand. When the priest was done, she stepped forward and thanked the others for coming, then spoke about her enduring affection for her husband. I heard some sniffling in the otherwise quiet crowd.

Not once in Rie's talk did she mention or express any hatred toward the killer. To me, that was a surer sign of her wrath and sadness than any other.

The coffin was carried out, and as the mourners began to shuffle home, I noticed someone I'd been expecting to see. She was walking alone.

I called out as she left the temple, "Miss Fujio?"

Miyako Fujio stopped and turned, her long hair whipping around. "You are . . . ?"

"We met in Hidaka's office the other day."

"I remember."

"My name is Nonoguchi, I'm Hidaka's friend. And I was a classmate of your brother's."

"So I heard. Hidaka told me after you left."

"I was wondering if we could talk? Do you have time?"

She looked down at her watch, then off into the distance. "Someone's waiting for me."

I followed her eyes. A light green van was parked along the side of the road. The young man sitting in the driver's seat was looking in our direction.

"Your husband?"

"No, not that."

Then, her lover, I assumed.

"We can just talk here. There's a few things I wanted to ask you."

"Like what?"

"I wanted to know what you talked about with Hidaka that day."

"What we always talked about. Recalling as many of the books as possible, admitting his wrongdoing in public, and re-writing the story so it had nothing to do with my brother. I had heard he was leaving for Canada and wanted to know exactly how he was going to show his sincere apologies once he'd left."

"And what did Hidaka say to that?"

"He said he would still respond in good faith, but he had no intentions of compromising his own beliefs to do so."

"So he wasn't going to go along with your requests?"

"Apparently he felt that as long as the intent was not an

exposé, but the attainment of art, that some intrusion on his subjects' privacy was unavoidable."

"But you didn't agree."

"Of course not." Her face softened slightly, but nothing you could remotely call a smile appeared.

"So you didn't get what you wanted that day."

"He said that as soon as he was settled in Canada, he would contact me, and we could continue where we left off. He promised. He did look like he was busy getting ready to relocate, and I didn't see any use pushing it, so I agreed and left."

I myself couldn't imagine anything else Hidaka could've said.

"And you went straight home?"

"Me? Yes."

"You didn't stop anywhere along the way?"

"No." She shook her head. Then Miyako Fujio's eyes opened a little wider and she stared hard at me. "Are you checking my alibi?"

"No, of course not." I dropped my eyes. If I wasn't checking her alibi, what was I doing? I started to wonder myself.

She sighed. "A detective visited me the other day and asked the same questions you're asking me now. Except he was a little more obvious about it. He wanted to know if I bore any malice toward Mr. Hidaka."

"Right." I looked up at her. "What did you tell him?"

"I told him I bore him no ill will at all. I just wanted him to respect the dead."

"So it's safe to say that you didn't like *Forbidden Hunting Grounds*? You feel it offends the memory of your brother?"

"Everyone has secrets. And everyone has the right to keep them. Even if they're dead."

"What if somebody felt those secrets were moving? Do you think it's such a bad thing to share that emotion with the world?"

"Emotion?" She stared at me curiously. Then she slowly shook her head. "What about a middle-school student who rapes a girl could possibly be moving?"

"Some things have to be said as the backdrop to a moving story."

She sighed again. For my benefit. "You're a writer, too, aren't you, Mr. Nonoguchi?"

"Yes, well, I write children's books."

"And are you so eager to defend Hidaka because you're an author yourself?"

I thought a moment before answering, "Maybe so."

"What a terrible profession." She looked back at her watch. "I'm sorry, I have to go." She turned and walked toward the waiting van.

I went back to my apartment building, where I found a piece of paper in my mailbox.

"I'm at the restaurant where we ate the other day. Give me a call. Kaga."

A phone number I assumed was the restaurant's was written at the bottom.

I changed out of my mourning clothes and went straight to the restaurant without calling. He was sitting by the window reading a book. I couldn't see what the title was.

He noticed me and started to stand. I waved him back down into his seat. "Don't bother."

"Sorry to call you out here like this." He lowered his head. He was aware that today was Hidaka's funeral.

I ordered another hot milk from the waitress and sat down.

"I know what you're after. This, right?" I pulled some folded sheets of paper out of my jacket pocket and set them down in front of him. These were the most recent notes, which I'd printed out before leaving home.

"Thanks so much." He reached out and unfolded the pages.

"Actually, could you not read it here? If you read the earlier notes, you know that I wrote about you, too. It would be embarrassing for you to read it in front of me."

He grinned. "Of course. I'll just put these away for now then." He refolded the pages and put them in his own jacket pocket.

"So," I asked after a sip of water, "I hope my notes are a little bit of help?"

"Oh, they are," Kaga said immediately. "There are things you can't pick up about the atmosphere of the case just by listening to stories, but when you see it all written down, it's easier to grasp. I wish the witnesses in my other cases would write down everything like this."

"Well, I'm glad."

The waitress brought my hot milk. It came with a spoon to scoop off the layer of froth on the top.

"What did you think about the cat?" I asked.

"I was surprised. You hear about cats causing trouble, but I don't think I'd ever heard about somebody taking it quite so far in dealing with one."

"Are you investigating the owner?"

"I made the reports to my boss, and someone else is on it."

"I see." I drank my milk. I didn't feel great about casting blame on someone else like that. "Well, other than that, I think everything in my notes is exactly as I told it to you."

"It was." He nodded. "But it's the details that have really helped."

"What kind of details?"

"Well, like the part where you were talking to Mr. Hidaka in his office. You wrote that Hidaka smoked one cigarette during that time. If we hadn't read your notes, we never would've known that."

"Yes . . . but just so you know, I'm not really sure it was only one. It could've been two. I just remember that he was smoking, so I wrote it like that."

"No, it was one cigarette," he said with finality. "No mistake."

"Okay."

I had no idea what that had to do with anything. Maybe it was just another example of the odd way that detectives saw the world.

I told Detective Kaga about speaking to Miyako Fujio after the funeral. He seemed intrigued by this.

"I never did get it out of her," I said, "but did she have an alibi?"

"Someone else is looking into that, but it looks like she does."

"I see. So I guess there's no point worrying about her too much then."

"Did you suspect her?"

"I wouldn't call it suspicion, but she did have a motive."

"You mean the intrusion into her brother's privacy? But killing Mr. Hidaka wouldn't fix that."

"What if she realized he wasn't going to be sincere about his apology, got mad, and killed him in the heat of the moment?"

"But Mr. Hidaka was still alive when she left the house."

"She could've come back later?"

"Intending to kill him?"

"Sure." I nodded. "Intending to kill him."

"But Rie was still in the house."

"She could've waited for her to leave, then sneaked in."

"So Miyako Fujio knew that Rie would be leaving the house before her husband did?"

"It might have come up in conversation."

Detective Kaga interlaced his fingers on the tabletop. He tapped the tips of his thumbs together repeatedly as he thought. After a while he said, "Did she come in through the front door?"

"How about the window?"

"So a woman in a suit came in through the window?" He grinned. "And Mr. Hidaka just sat there, watching her?"

"She could've just waited until he'd gone to the bathroom. Then waited behind the door for him to come back."

"The paperweight in her hand?" Detective Kaga swung his right fist up and down.

"I suppose so. Then Hidaka walks in"—I made a fist of

my right hand, too—"and she smacks him in the back of the head."

"I see. And after that?"

I thought back on what Detective Kaga had told me the other day. "Then I guess she strangled him. With the telephone cord, right? Then she fled the scene."

"How did she leave?"

"Out the window. If she'd gone out the front door, it would've been unlocked when we got there later."

"That's true." He reached out for his coffee cup, noticed it was empty, and left the empty cup sitting there. "But why didn't she go out the front door?"

"I don't know. Maybe she didn't want people to see her? Perhaps it was a psychological thing. Of course, if she has an alibi anyway, this is all just fanciful conjecture."

"True enough. She does have an alibi, which would indeed make the story you just told entirely fanciful conjecture."

Something about the deliberate way he repeated my own words struck me as odd. "You can go ahead and forget it then."

"Still, it was an interesting scenario. I was wondering if you could make another guess for me."

"I'm not terribly good at this, but sure. Fire away."

"Why did the killer turn off the lights in the room before leaving?"

"Isn't it obvious?" I said after a moment's thought. "She wanted people to think no one was home. That way, even if anyone happened by, they would just leave. It would delay the discovery of the body. Which is, in fact, what did happen."

"So the killer wanted to delay the discovery of the body?"

"Don't all killers want to do that?"

"Maybe," he said. "If that was the plan, then why was the computer left on?"

"The computer?"

"Yes. When you came into the room, the screen was on. It was in your account."

"That's true. Maybe she didn't care whether the computer was on or not."

"I tried a simple experiment after leaving you the other day. We turned off all the lights in the room and left on the computer monitor. It turns out it's quite bright. You can see it dimly through the curtains even standing outside the room. If she really wanted to make it look like no one was home, she would've turned off the computer."

"Maybe she couldn't find the switch. People who aren't familiar with computers don't know about those kinds of things."

"She could've at least turned off the monitor. The switch is right there on the front. And if she didn't understand that, she could've pulled the cord."

"I guess she forgot."

Detective Kaga stared at me for a moment, then nodded. "That's probably it. She probably forgot."

Having nothing else to say to that, I remained silent.

He stood, thanking me again for my time. "Will you be writing about today in your account as well?"

"I expect I will."

"Then I'll be able to read it?"

"Fine by me."

He headed toward the cash register, then stopped midway. "Did you really think I wasn't cut out to be a teacher?"

I remembered writing something along those lines in my account. "That's just my opinion."

He looked down again, gave a brief sigh, and walked out.

I wondered what Kaga was thinking.

If he'd already figured out something about the case, I wondered why he didn't just tell me.

2

SUSPICION

KYOICHIRO KAGA'S NOTES

One of the things I took particular note of was the use of a paperweight as the murder weapon. I need hardly mention that the paperweight belonged to the late author and thus was in the office prior to the killing. This suggests that the killer didn't come to the house with the intent of killing Kunihiko Hidaka.

Had the murder been planned from the beginning, the murderer would have come prepared with a weapon. It's possible that such preparations had been made, but then unforeseen circumstances necessitated a change in plans, making a blow to the back of the head with the paperweight the next-best option. However, that seems rather poorly premeditated. It makes most sense that the murder was an impulsive act, done in the heat of the moment, with whatever implement was at hand.

This makes me wonder about the locked doors. According to the statements of the two who discovered the body, both the front door to the house and Kunihiko Hidaka's home office door were locked.

Rie Hidaka had this to say:

"When I left the house just after five o'clock, I locked the front door. I was worried that, since he was in his office, my husband might not hear it if somebody walked in. Of course, I never imagined anyone actually would."

According to forensics, only the Hidakas' fingerprints were found on the front doorknob. There were no signs of gloves having been used, or fingerprints being wiped off. I think it's safe to assume that the door was locked by Rie Hidaka when she left and it remained so until she opened it upon her return.

However, there's a high probability that the murderer locked the door to Mr. Hidaka's home office from the inside. Unlike the front door, the office-door handle showed clear signs of having been wiped clean.

This leads me to believe that the murderer did, in fact, come in through the office window. However, this would seem to create a contradiction. If the murder wasn't premeditated, why come in through the window? It's highly unlikely that the intruder intended to steal anything. Even a thief seeing the house for the first time would soon realize there was nothing left worth stealing.

However, one line of conjecture resolves this contradiction. What if we assume that the killer visited the Hidaka household twice in the same day? The first time, the killer came in the front door as a guest. Then, after leaving the house (or, rather, pretending to leave), the killer returned, this time entering through the window with a single purpose in mind. That purpose, I need hardly say, was to kill Kunihiko Hidaka. It makes the most sense to assume that this impulse to murder stemmed from something that happened during the killer's first visit.

Now we must consider who visited the Hidaka household on the day of the murder. At present, we know of two people: Miyako Fujio and Osamu Nonoguchi.

At the beginning of our investigation, we focused on these two as the prime suspects. We were somewhat astonished to find that both of them had alibis.

Miyako Fujio had returned to her home by six o'clock the evening of the day in question. We have two witnesses corroborating this: her fiancé, Tadao Nakazuka, and a man who was going to assist with their wedding, Kikuo Ueda. They were meeting to discuss the couple's nuptials, to be held next month. Ueda is Nakazuka's boss at work, with no direct personal connection to Miyako Fujio. It is difficult to imagine that he would falsify his account to cover for his subordinate's fiancée. Furthermore, according to Rie Hidaka, Miyako Fujio left the Hidaka household a little after five o'clock, which, considering the transportation routes and distance between the Hidaka and Fujio houses means an arrival time of six o'clock makes perfect sense. We have to conclude that her alibi is sound.

Now, for Osamu Nonoguchi.

I can't deny that I have some personal feelings concerning this individual. He was a colleague at my former position, and as such he knew me during those less-than-happy days.

Were our personal connection to cast a shadow on my investigation in any way, I'd be obliged to remove myself from the case. However, I'm determined to view our shared history as objectively as possible while continuing to pursue this case. Note that I don't intend to forget said history. For I believe that history could prove an important weapon going forward.

The following is Mr. Nonoguchi's alibi for the day in question:

Having been visiting at the Hidakas', he left around four thirty in the afternoon shortly after Miyako Fujio arrived. He went straight home and worked until around six o'clock. At that time, his editor from Dojisha Publishing, a Mr. Yukio Oshima, arrived and they began their meeting. Soon after, a call came from Kunihiko Hidaka, saying he wanted to talk about something, and asking Mr. Nonoguchi to come to his house at eight o'clock.

Nonoguchi and Oshima went to a nearby restaurant and ate, after which Nonoguchi left for the Hidaka household. He arrived just around eight o'clock to find the house apparently empty. Growing suspicious, he phoned Rie Hidaka. He then waited in the Lamp, a nearby café. He returned to the Hidaka household at around eight forty, just as Rie Hidaka was arriving. Together they went inside and discovered the body in Hidaka's home office, accessible via a hallway from the living room.

Taking all of this at face value, Osamu Nonoguchi's alibi seems nearly perfect. Mr. Oshima from Dojisha Publishing and the owner of the Lamp both corroborate his story.

However, it's not entirely ironclad. Even assuming his account is mostly accurate, he would have had an opportunity to kill Kunihiko Hidaka before phoning Rie. To do this, he would have had to go straight from dinner with Mr. Oshima to the Hidaka household, immediately kill Mr. Hidaka, then, after covering his tracks, blithely phone the victim's wife as though nothing had happened.

However, according to the autopsy, this scenario doesn't work. For lunch that day, while out shopping with his wife, Kunihiko Hidaka had eaten a hamburger, and from the state of digestion, we can say that the time of death was between five and six in the afternoon, and certainly no later than seven.

Osamu Nonoguchi's alibi holds.

However, I still suspect he is the murderer. My reason for this is something he said on the night of the murder. Something that, from the moment I heard it, made me consider the possibility that he was the killer. Though I understand it is extremely inefficient to operate on a gut feeling, I decided to give intuition the reins, if only this once.

That Osamu Nonoguchi was keeping a record of the case came as a great surprise to me. Were he the killer, it would be against his best interest to make known any details about the case. However, when I read his account, I realized he had exactly the opposite goal in mind.

The account is written in an orderly fashion, and this very orderliness gives it persuasive power. As you read it, you forget that the events it portrays might not necessarily be the truth. Therein lies Nonoguchi's aim: to create a fictional account of the events in order to divert suspicion from himself.

He must have realized it was only a matter of time before he became a suspect. He was looking for a way out when who should appear before him but someone he knew—a man who used to be a teacher at the same school. He decided to use this man by writing a false account and giving it to him to read. Nonoguchi probably reasoned that since the man hadn't been much of a teacher, he probably wasn't much of a detective either and would easily be taken in by his trick.

Perhaps I'm reading too much into this. Perhaps I am trying so hard to keep my personal feelings out of the investigation that I am blinding myself to the truth. Still, in his written account, I discovered several traps carefully laid for the unwary reader. Then, ironically, I found vital evidence in that very account proving that he, and only he, could be the killer.

I carefully went back over my own line of conjecture and, when I was satisfied, made my report. My superior in Homicide is meticulous and cautious, but he agreed with my line of reasoning. In fact, from the very first time they'd met, he, too, had suspected Osamu Nonoguchi. Though Nonoguchi's account doesn't mention this, the night of the murder he seemed excited and unusually talkative. Both my superior and I recognized this as one of the classic indications of guilt.

"The problem," my superior said, "is evidence."

I couldn't agree more. Though I was confident that my scenario was correct, it was based entirely on circumstantial evidence.

There was another problem: motive. Though I gathered no small amount of information on both Kunihiko Hidaka and Osamu Nonoguchi, I couldn't find any reason, none whatsoever, for Nonoguchi to bear him any malice. To the contrary, if anything, Nonoguchi should have been grateful, considering how Hidaka had helped him advance his career as a writer.

I reflected back on the Osamu Nonoguchi I knew from our time together as teachers. As a composition teacher in middle school, he'd struck me as a man who kept a cool head and performed his assigned task without much error or deviation. Even when something unexpected happened, such as trouble with a student, he never got ruffled. Instead, he would refer back to the records of any similar events and use them as a guide to the course of action least likely to cause difficulties. He was good at this. To put it less generously, he avoided making decisions on his own and played everything by the book. A former colleague had this to say:

"Mr. Nonoguchi never really wanted to be a teacher, you

know. He plays it cool like that because he doesn't want to waste time actually worrying about his students or take on any responsibility beyond his basic duties. That's why he doesn't get involved."

Her theory was that Nonoguchi wanted to quit as soon as possible and become a full-time writer. He never went to faculty parties and the like because he was at home writing.

Osamu Nonoguchi did indeed quit teaching and become an author; yet it remains unclear what he really thought of being a teacher.

My only insight comes from something he told me once:

"The relationship between teacher and student is based on illusion. The teacher is under the illusion that he is teaching something, and the student is under the illusion that he is being taught. What's important is that this shared illusion makes both teacher and student happy. Nothing good is gained by facing the truth, after all. All we're doing is playing at education."

One wonders what could have happened to make him think such a thing.

3

RESOLUTION

OSAMU NONOGUCHI'S ACCOUNT

etective Kaga has given me special permission to complete the following account before I leave the room I currently occupy. Why I asked to be allowed to do so is, I'm sure, incomprehensible to him. I doubt he'd understand even if I told him that it was a writer's basic instinct to want to finish a piece he'd started, even if it was begun under false pretenses.

Yet I believe that my experiences over the past hour or so are worthy of recording. This, too, I credit to writer's instinct—though what I write is the story of my ruination.

Detective Kaga arrived today, April 21, at precisely ten in the morning. The instant the bell rang, I had a feeling that it was him, a premonition soon confirmed when I looked through the peephole. Still, I made an effort to conceal my agitation as I welcomed him in.

"Sorry to drop in so suddenly," he said in his customary calm tone. "There was something I wanted to discuss."

"What is that?" I asked, inviting him in.

I showed him to the sofa and offered him tea. He said not to bother, but I made it anyway.

"So what's this about?" I said, placing the teacup in front

of him. I noticed that my hand was trembling. I glanced up to see Detective Kaga looking at my hand.

He didn't touch his tea. "Actually," he said, staring straight at me, "I've come to say something extremely difficult."

"Yes?" I was desperately trying to remain calm, when in fact my heart was racing so fast, I thought I might pass out at any moment.

"I'm going to have to ask you to let me search your apartment."

I tried a look of astonishment, then let it fade into what I hoped was a natural-looking smile. I'm not sure whether the performance worked. To Kaga, I'm afraid it probably just looked like a grimace.

"What's this about? You're not going to find anything here."

"I wish that were true, but I'm afraid I will."

"Wait a second. Let me get this straight: You think I killed Hidaka? And you think you're going to find evidence of that here?"

Detective Kaga gave a short nod. "Essentially, yes."

"Well, this is a surprise," I lied. I shook my head and attempted a little sigh. This performance was already straining the limits of my abilities. "I'm not sure what to say, this is so unexpected. That is, unless you're joking? But . . . you're not, are you."

"No, I'm afraid I'm quite serious. As much as it pains me to have to say that to a former colleague, I have a duty to uncover the truth, wherever it may lie."

"I understand your job, and I know that any reasonable suspicion, even if it involves a good friend or close relative, has to be investigated. But, to be honest, I'm surprised and more than a little bewildered. It's all so sudden."

"I've brought a warrant."

"A search warrant? I'm sure you have. But before you start waving it around, maybe you can tell me why it's come to this? I mean—"

"Why I suspect you?"

"Yes, I guess that's it. Or do you normally just start rooting through someone's stuff without so much as a word of explanation?"

"Sometimes, if necessary." He looked down at the table, then finally reached for his cup and took a sip of tea. Then he looked back at me. "But I'd be happy to explain it to you."

"Well, I'm much obliged. Though I can't promise I'll see things the same way you do."

Kaga pulled a notebook out of his jacket pocket. "The most important point is the time of death. We understand that Kunihiko Hidaka was killed somewhere between five and seven o'clock, but according to the coroner, it is extremely unlikely he died after six. Estimating the time of death by examining the state of digestion of food is a very reliable method, and in a case like this, it can usually narrow the time of death down to a smaller window of time than two hours. Yet we have a witness who testifies that Hidaka was alive after six o'clock."

"Well, it's the truth. What do you want me to say? I realize the possibility is slight, but we're talking natural processes here. Would it really be that astonishing if the doctor was twenty or thirty minutes off?"

"Of course not, but what concerns us is that the basis of this testimony was a phone call. We can't be sure that it was really Hidaka on the phone."

"Oh, no, I'm sure it was Hidaka. Without question."

"Yes, but you can't prove that. No one except you was on that phone call."

"I guess you'll just have to take my word for it."

"I would like to do that—I would; but your word won't hold up in court."

"Well . . . I did answer the phone, yes, but don't forget there was a person standing right next to me at the time. You talked to Mr. Oshima from Dojisha about this, didn't you?"

"We did. He confirmed that you received a call shortly after six."

"Didn't he hear us talking?"

"No, he only heard you. He said it sounded like you made arrangements to meet someone. And that afterward, you told him the person you were talking to was Kunihiko Hidaka."

"So how doesn't that qualify as proof? Is it that you think someone else called me and I just made it sound like it was from Hidaka? Is that what you're getting at?"

Kaga frowned and chewed his lower lip for a moment before replying. "The possibility can't be ruled out entirely."

"Well, I wish it could, because it doesn't look like you're much for taking someone at his word." I made a show of being offended. "What I don't get is why you're so hung up on the time of death. Sure, it might be a little off from what the autopsy says, but not by much. Yet from what you're saying, it sounds like if it strays a few minutes in the wrong direction, then I've just made the whole thing up. I hope you have a better reason for doubting me, because if not, frankly, it's insulting."

Kaga stared me in the eye for a long moment before responding, "I do have a better reason."

"Well, let's hear it."

"The cigarette."

"Excuse me?"

"You told me that Mr. Hidaka was a heavy smoker, to the point where it sometimes felt like he was fumigating his office."

"What of it?" I felt an ugly premonition, like black smoke, spreading to fill my chest.

"There was only one cigarette butt in the ashtray."

I gasped despite myself.

"One cigarette butt, thoroughly mangled. If he'd done any work after Miyako Fujio went home a little after five, there should've been others. Furthermore, the one cigarette that was there wasn't one he smoked while he was working. He smoked it while he was talking to you, Mr. Nonoguchi. You said as much in your account."

I dimly recalled Kaga mentioning something about the number of cigarettes Hidaka had smoked. Had he been onto me this whole time?

"In other words," he continued, "from the time that Miyako Fujio left Hidaka alone to the time that he was killed, he didn't smoke even one cigarette. I mentioned this to the wife, and she told me that even if he'd only been working for thirty minutes, he'd have smoked at least two or three. She said he also had a tendency to smoke more when he was starting work on a new installment. And yet, that night he didn't smoke a single cigarette. What am I to make of this?"

I had already begun inwardly chastising myself. It was so obvious, yet it had never crossed my mind. Probably because I don't smoke.

"Maybe he was out of cigarettes?" I tried, realizing this tactic was probably futile. "Or he realized he didn't have enough to last, so he was pacing himself?"

"That day at lunch, Hidaka bought four packs. A pack with fourteen cigarettes remained on his desk, and there were three unopened packs in his desk drawer."

Though Kaga spoke softly, I could feel his words slowly advancing toward me, each step powerful, inevitable. I remembered that he was good at kendo, and a shiver ran down my spine.

"Well, what do you know!" I said. "I guess that *would* make a single cigarette seem a little suspicious. Though you'd have to ask Hidaka himself why he didn't smoke more. Maybe he had a sore throat, or something like that?" It was a last, desperate line of defense.

"If that were the case, I wouldn't think he'd have smoked while you were there, either. I'm afraid we have to assume the most likely explanation."

"In other words, that he was killed earlier."

"Much earlier. In fact it only makes sense if he left his office just after Ms. Fujio departed, then, after his wife left for the hotel, he went back to his desk and was killed immediately."

"You seem pretty sure of that."

"Going back to the cigarette briefly, it's worth noting that Hidaka didn't even smoke one while Ms. Fujio was there—and with good reason. According to his wife, Ms. Fujio didn't like cigarette smoke, and he'd decided not to smoke while she was there, in hopes it would help smooth things out."

"No kidding." One thing I could say about Hidaka: he was always a shrewd tactician.

"And yet there is no doubt that his conversation with Ms. Fujio was stressful. One would assume that as soon as she left, and he was done speaking to his wife, he'd have lit up a cigarette with the eagerness of a starving man. Yet there are no butts. Did he not smoke? Could he not smoke? I believe it is the latter."

"Because he was killed."

"Yes." Kaga nodded.

"But I left the Hidaka's a long time before that."

"I know. You went out the front door. After which you went around to the garden, to Hidaka's office window."

"You say that like you were standing there watching me do it."

"Actually, it was you who gave me the idea, albeit while you were speculating that Miyako Fujio was the killer. In your version, she pretended to leave the Hidakas' and then went around to the office, did she not? I wondered if you weren't simply relating what you yourself had done."

I shook my head slowly. "Serves me right for trying to be helpful! I wouldn't have said a thing if I'd thought you were going to twist it around and throw it back at me like this."

Detective Kaga looked down at his notebook. "In your own account, you described your departure from the Hidakas' in the following manner: " 'Good-bye,' she said, and stood watching me until I'd turned the corner.' *She* here refers to Rie Hidaka."

"So? That's what happened."

"According to what you wrote, she went as far as the front gate to see you off. Yet when I talked to her about this, she said she only saw you as far as the front door. How do I explain this contradiction?"

"I wouldn't go so far as to call it a contradiction! One of us remembered events differently, that's all."

"Really? I don't think so. I think you purposely wrote a false account of what happened. You did this in order to camouflage the fact that you never went to the corner. You never even left the front gate."

I scoffed. "Ridiculous. You're dreaming this stuff up and trying to make it all fit. It's amazing what you can accomplish once you've drawn your conclusion in advance."

"Personally, I feel I'm approaching this case very objectively."

The look in his eyes made me flinch, even though my brain was off wondering about completely unrelated things, such as why this man loved saying *personally* all the time.

"Fine, whatever. You're free to make whatever conjectures you like. But while you're at it, I'd like you to paint the whole picture for me. What happened next? I was crouched beneath the window, and what then? Did I sneak in through the window and whack Hidaka?"

"Did you?" Detective Kaga looked directly at me.

"Hey, I'm asking you."

Kaga shook his head slightly. "I'm afraid only the one who did it knows all the details of the crime."

"What? Are you asking me to confess? Believe me, I'd be happy to—if I'd actually done it. But I didn't do it. Sorry to rain on your parade. Let's get back to the phone call, shall we? Remember, the one I got from Hidaka after you claim that he was killed? If that wasn't from Hidaka, who was it from? My story has been reported widely in the press. If someone else happened to have called me around then, wouldn't they have gone to the police by now?" I stuck up a finger as though I'd just had a thought. "Wait, you think I had a conspirator, don't you! You think I had someone call me on purpose."

Kaga looked around the room without answering. His eyes eventually came to rest on the cordless phone sitting on the dining-room table. He went over, picked it up, and then came back to the sofa.

"You didn't need a conspirator. All you needed was for this phone to ring."

"But how does the phone ring if no one's calling?" I clapped my hands. "Wait! I see what you're getting at. You think I was carrying a cell phone in my pocket. Then, when Oshima wasn't looking, I called my own home phone. Right?"

"That would be one way to do it."

"Fine, but that's impossible. I don't have a cell phone, and I don't know anyone I could have borrowed one from. Besides, couldn't you just check the records? I'm sure the telephone company would be able to see if I'd called my own phone number."

"Actually, it turns out to be very difficult to run a reverse trace and look up where a phone call came from."

"Ah, is that what it's called—a reverse trace?"

"However, that isn't necessary, since it's very easy to tell who a particular phone call was made to. All we need to do in this case is check and see where Mr. Hidaka called that day."

"And did you?"

"We did." Kaga nodded.

"I already know the answer, but tell me, what did you find?"

"We found a record of a call from his house to your apartment at six thirteen."

"Of course you did. Because he called me and we spoke." I tried to appear confident even though my fear was growing by the moment. If the phone company record hadn't been enough to dispel Kaga's suspicions, then he was onto my trick.

Kaga stood and returned the cordless phone to the table. This time, however, he didn't come back to the sofa. "Hidaka was supposed to send his finished manuscript by fax. However, there's no fax machine in his office. I'm sure you know why."

I almost said that I didn't, but I held my tongue instead.

"Because he could send it directly from his computer, right?" Kaga asked.

"I've heard that can be done."

"It's very convenient for people who still need to send faxes. You don't have to keep paper at hand, for one thing. Of course, Hidaka was going to switch to sending in his submissions by e-mail once he was in Canada. He'd already asked his editor to make any necessary adjustments for this on their end."

"I don't know about any of that. I don't use computers much. All I know is that Hidaka once mentioned something about sending faxes directly from his computer."

"There's nothing difficult about it. Anyone can do it. And the software comes with lots of useful features. You can send to several different numbers simultaneously if you want, and you can save a list of common recipients. Also"—Kaga paused, looking down at me—"if you set the time, you can have it send a fax automatically."

I looked at the floor, away from his eyes. "And you think that's what I did?"

He didn't answer the question. There was no need.

"It was the lights that bothered me at first," he said. "You said all the lights were out when you arrived at the Hidakas'. The killer had probably wanted to make it look like Hidaka had gone out, though you couldn't figure out why they had left the computer on, correct? I think I know why. Because the computer was necessary for the fax trick to work. It had to be left on. After you killed Hidaka, you scrambled to create an alibi. Specifically, you turned on his computer, pulled up some suitable document, and set the computer to fax that document to you at 6:13 p.m. Then you went around and turned off every light in the house, a necessary step for the story you were going to tell. If you were going to return to the house at eight o'clock, think Hidaka wasn't home, and then go so far as to call his hotel, you needed the lights to be off. Even if the lights had been on only in that one room, you would have come around and looked through Hidaka's office window before calling the hotel. And you wanted Rie Hidaka to be there with you when you discovered the body."

After this little speech Kaga paused. Perhaps he was waiting for me to retort or attempt an explanation. I remained quiet.

"I think you probably considered the computer monitor yourself," he went on after a moment. "As I said previously, the monitor puts out quite a bit of light. But the PC needed to be running. You could've turned off just the monitor, but that would've been dangerous. Rie was with you when you discovered the body, and if she had noticed that the computer was running but the monitor was turned off, that might've been enough to tip off the police to your trick right there on the spot."

I tried to swallow, but my mouth was completely dry. I realized I was terrified of meeting Kaga's eyes. He had seen right through my flimsy layers of subterfuge, right through my skull and down into the very thoughts that had been in my head.

"I'm guessing you left the Hidakas' around five thirty. On your way back to your apartment, you stopped and called Mr. Oshima at Dojisha Publishing and asked him to come over right away to pick up your latest manuscript. Mr. Oshima had been expecting the manuscript by fax that day and was surprised by the sudden, urgent request to see him. Luckily for you, it's a straight shot on the train from his office and he was able to make it to your apartment in thirty minutes. I noted that none of this was mentioned in your account. In fact, from what you wrote, it seemed as if Mr. Oshima had been intending to come that day all along."

This, too, was true, but instead of saying anything, I just gave a long sigh.

"I hardly need to go into why you called Mr. Oshima over. You needed someone to corroborate your alibi. Hidaka's computer called your house at exactly six thirteen, like you'd set it up to do. You'd turned off your own fax machine before then so you could take the call on your cordless phone. You picked up the receiver to listen to the scrambled noises of Mr. Hidaka's fax program attempting to make a connection and then began your greatest performance. With electronic noise warbling in your ear, you begin talking as though you were speaking to another human. I call your performance great because, in fact, Mr. Oshima was completely taken in by it. After you had finished your solo one-act play, you hung up. On Hidaka's computer's side, the call was logged as a dialing error, and the job was suspended. Now, all that was left for you was a little cleanup. You merely had to discover the body with Rie Hidaka by your side. Then, before the police arrived, when she wasn't looking, you needed to erase the record of the call off the computer."

I noticed that somewhere along the way, he'd stopped reflexively bowing his head every time he said something. That bowing was the habit of a new recruit at school when speaking to a senior colleague. The change in attitude didn't bother me, though. It was fitting given the facts of our current relationship.

"It was a decent trick. Even more impressive because you came up with it in such a short amount of time. However, you made one mistake."

I had a feeling he was about to tell me what that was.

"You forgot about the real phone at the Hidakas'. If Mr. Hidaka had actually phoned you, then pressing the redial button on his phone should call this apartment."

Inwardly, I screamed.

"Yet it didn't. It called a place in Vancouver. According to the wife, Mr. Hidaka had placed a call early that morning, around six in the morning, to Canada. Of course, it might be possible to explain that one away. After he'd called your apartment, he could have attempted to call Canada only to hang up before actually letting the call go through. However, considering the time difference, that doesn't make much sense. Someone who had gotten up especially early to make a phone call that very morning wouldn't likely forget the time difference and mistakenly call again in the middle of the night."

Kaga stopped talking and gazed at me. "That's all."

For a brief moment nothing was said between us. If Kaga was waiting for me to react, he was going to have to wait a long time. My mind was a blank.

"Nothing to say?" He sounded somewhat surprised.

Finally, I looked up and our eyes met. His were calm, unthreatening—not the look a detective would turn upon a suspect. That came as a relief, irrational though that may be.

"You never said anything about the manuscript," I said. "What about the episode of *The Gates of Ice* on Hidaka's computer? Even pretending your theory is correct so far, when did he write that?"

Tight-lipped, Detective Kaga looked up at the ceiling. I got the sense that he already knew what he was going to say, he was merely finding the right words to say it.

Finally, he spoke. "There are two possibilities. The first is that Mr. Hidaka had already written that much, and when you found that on his computer, you decided to use it to support your alibi."

"And the other possibility?"

"The other one"—he looked back at me—"is that you wrote that manuscript. You could've had it with you on a disk and, in order to create your alibi, hurriedly copied it onto Hidaka's computer."

"That's quite the theory!" I tried to smile, but my cheeks were too tight and my face felt frozen.

"I showed the manuscript file to a Mr. Yamabe at *Somei Monthly*, Hidaka's publisher. According to him, it was clearly written by someone other than Mr. Hidaka. The wording was slightly different, and there were too many variances in things like line breaks and formatting."

"So, er, you . . ." My voice came out in a hoarse rasp. I coughed to clear my throat. "You think I prepared that manuscript in advance because I was intending to kill him?"

"No, I don't think that. Had you planned to use it to stand in for his work, you would've taken greater pains to match his style and format. His editor thought that wouldn't be a terribly difficult thing to do for such a short section of a work that was already partially published. Also, given that a paperweight was the murder weapon, and that Mr. Oshima was summoned at the last minute to corroborate your alibi, I have to conclude that the murder was done on impulse."

"So then why prepare the manuscript ahead of time?"

"That's the question, isn't it? Why did you have in your possession a manuscript for the next installment of *The Gates of Ice*? And even before we ask that question, we need to ask why you'd written it in the first place. I'm very intrigued by this point in particular. I think that in the answer to that question lies your motive for killing Mr. Hidaka."

I closed my eyes to avoid full-blown panic. "This is all in your imagination. You have no proof."

"True. That's why I'm here today to search your apartment. I'm sure you know by now what it is I'm looking for."

I didn't answer.

"I'm looking for a disk containing the manuscript. Or perhaps I'll find it on the hard drive of your word processor over there. In fact, I'm sure I will. If you'd only prepared the manuscript as part of an elaborate murder plan, you would have destroyed the evidence. But I don't believe that. No, it's definitely here, somewhere."

I opened my eyes to find Kaga staring directly at me. Except this time I was able to accept his gaze without flinching. All it took was closing my eyes for a moment to settle myself completely.

"And if you find what you're looking for, you're going to arrest me?"

"I'm afraid so, yes."

"What if I chose to turn myself in now?"

Kaga's eyes went wide. He shook his head once. "Unfortunately, we're past the point where it would be considered turning yourself in. Though I wouldn't advise any attempts to resist arrest."

"I see." The strength left my shoulders. I felt despair; yet also a kind of relief. I no longer had to pretend. "When did you first suspect me?"

"The first night."

"Really! Did I slip up?"

"You did." He nodded. "You asked me about the estimated time of death."

"Is that so strange?"

"Very. If you spoke with Mr. Hidaka after six o'clock and knew he'd been killed before you reached the house at eight o'clock, then the murder would've taken place during that short two-hour period. Why go out of your way to ask what you already knew?"

"Oh."

"Also, the next day, at that restaurant, you asked me the same question again. Then I was even more certain that my hunch was correct: You didn't want to know what time the crime had occurred. You wanted to know what time the police *thought* the crime had occurred."

He was correct. I'd been checking to see whether my trick had worked.

"Well, that's fantastic. I think you're probably a very good detective."

"Thank you." He bowed his head curtly. "You might want to get ready to leave. Though I will have to keep a close watch on you. There are plenty of cases where a suspect has been left alone with unpleasant results."

"Don't worry, I'm not going to commit suicide." I laughed. The last came naturally, surprising even me.

"I should hope not," Kaga said with a smile.

4

PURSUIT

KYOICHIRO KAGA'S NOTES

Four days have passed since I arrested Osamu Nonoguchi. Though he admitted the crime, his lips remain tightly sealed on one matter: his motive. Why did he kill a man who was his childhood friend and a benefactor? The chief has made it clear that, without a clear motive, we can't bring this case to trial. Nonoguchi might recant his confession, and his lawyer might poke enough holes in our circumstantial evidence to create reasonable doubt. The chance that everything could fall apart in court is too great.

Yet despite repeated questioning, all he would say was "I just got angry and killed him in the heat of the moment. That's all."

This wasn't nearly enough for us to establish motive, but I did have an inkling of the real motive. My first clue was the manuscript for *The Gates of Ice*.

I should mention that we did find the manuscript as I'd expected, on the hard drive of Mr. Nonoguchi's word processor. Also, in his desk drawer, we found the disk he'd brought to the Hidakas' on the day of the murder, which was, indeed, compatible with the disk drive of the computer in Kunihiko Hidaka's office.

Yet I don't believe this was a premeditated murder—an opinion shared by the entire investigation team. Which raises the question of why, that very day, Mr. Nonoguchi just happened to be carrying the next installment of *The Gates of Ice* on a disk in his pocket. And before we ask even that question, we need to know why Mr. Nonoguchi had written a manuscript for a work that was supposed to be Hidaka's.

I had a working theory about this point in particular, even before I made the arrest. I was convinced that if I could trace this theory back to its logical origins, I would find the motive for this murder.

All that remained was to get Mr. Nonoguchi to corroborate my theory; but he proved uncooperative. Regarding the manuscript for *The Gates of Ice*, he said, "I wrote it on a lark. I brought it to Hidaka's to surprise him. I told him if he wasn't going to make his deadline, he could always use my version. Of course, he took it as the joke it was meant to be."

I need hardly point out that this story was unconvincing. Yet when pressed further, the suspect simply said that it was my choice whether to believe him.

My team searched Mr. Nonoguchi's apartment again, having examined only his desk and the word processor's hard drive the first time around.

The second search resulted in eighteen pieces of evidence, including eight thick, spiral-bound notebooks, eight double-density floppy disks, and two file folders containing short, handwritten manuscripts. All of these contained numerous pieces of fiction, both short stories and novels. We confirmed that the handwriting in the spiral-bound notebooks and on the handwritten manuscripts all belonged to Mr. Nonoguchi.

What was of particular interest was the content of the writings. One of the floppies contained something startling— though if my theory is correct, entirely expected. This was a manuscript for *The Gates of Ice*. Not just the latest installment, but every installment that had been published so far.

I showed the manuscripts to Mr. Yamabe, Hidaka's editor at *Somei Monthly*. His opinion:

"This is, without a doubt, a manuscript for *The Gates of Ice* as published. That said, even though the story is more or less the same, there are a few things in here that weren't in the manuscripts I received from Mr. Hidaka. And others seem to be missing. Again, the word use and sentence structure is slightly different."

In other words, these earlier installments showed the same differences from the printed version as the manuscript Nonoguchi attempted to use as part of his alibi.

The investigation team then obtained copies of every printed work of Kunihiko Hidaka's, divided them up, and read them. (Several people on the team commented that it had been a long while since they'd read so much, and there was belly-aching all around.)

We discovered that the five full-length novels written in the spiral-bound notebooks in Osamu Nonoguchi's apartment all closely matched works published by Kunihiko Hidaka. Despite slight differences in the titles, characters' names, and settings, the general story lines were practically identical.

The floppy disks contained three more novels and twenty short stories, of which all the novels and seventeen of the short stories matched works by Mr. Hidaka. The three short stories that didn't match were children's stories that had been published by Mr. Nonoguchi.

As for the two short, handwritten works, no corresponding publications were found in Mr. Hidaka's output. Based on the age of the paper, these appeared to have been written some time ago. Perhaps if we expanded the scope of our investigation, we might find something.

Finding so many manuscripts for works by another author was highly unusual. Moreover, the manuscripts were not identical to their published versions. The stories written in the spiral-bound notebooks had several notes in the margins and corrections had been made, making them seem more like works in progress than something finished.

My theory is that Osamu Nonoguchi had been working as Kunihiko Hidaka's ghostwriter. I suspect that something in that relationship soured, leading to the present situation.

I proposed my theory to Nonoguchi in the interrogation room, but he flatly denied it: "You're wrong."

When I asked him about the stories in those spiral notebooks and floppy disks, he closed his eyes and fell silent. The investigator in the room with me tried to badger it out of him, but he wouldn't talk.

That was as far as we were able to get—day after day, session after session—then today, in the middle of the interrogation session, something unexpected happened.

Osamu Nonoguchi suddenly put a hand to his stomach and complained of a sharp pain. The attack was so sudden and so severe, I was afraid he'd somehow smuggled in some poison and taken it.

He was taken to the police hospital immediately and given a full examination. The chief called me in shortly after with startling news: Osamu Nonoguchi has cancer.

I went to visit him in the hospital the day after he collapsed in the questioning room, first speaking briefly with the physician in charge of his case.

According to the doctor, the cancer had spread to the membrane around his internal organs. This was a dangerous phase of his cancer, and if he was to have any hope of surviving, it would require immediate surgery.

When I asked the doctor if the cancer was new or a recurrence after a remission, he told me that it likely was a relapse.

This news wasn't a surprise. In our investigation, we'd learned that, two years prior, Osamu Nonoguchi had to have a portion of his stomach removed due to cancer and been forced to take several months off from his teaching job.

Nonoguchi hadn't been back to the hospital until now, after he was arrested, even though, as the doctor told me now, he had probably known about the return of his cancer for some time.

I then asked the doctor if surgery would save Nonoguchi's life. The doctor pondered this for a while, then finally shrugged. "I give him a fifty-fifty chance."

That wasn't the answer I wanted.

I took my leave of the doctor and went to visit Osamu Nonoguchi.

He was in a private room. "I feel bad that I get to lounge about here in the lap of luxury instead of going to prison," he said with a weak smile, from his hospital bed. I realized it was more than just years that had aged his thin face since the time we'd been colleagues.

"How do you feel?"

"Not good, but considering the nature of my illness, I'd have to say I'm doing pretty well."

I sat silent, next to his bed, for a while, until he turned to me and asked, "When will I be put on trial? If it takes too long, I might not make it."

I was unsure if he was joking, though he had clearly already accepted that his death was inevitable and fast approaching.

"The trial won't happen for a while. We don't have enough evidence and detail to start."

"Why not? I've confessed, and you have proof. Put me on trial and you'll get a guilty verdict. Isn't that enough? I promise I won't change my story when I'm on the stand."

"Actually, I wish you would change your story. Right now, it lacks a motive."

"That again?"

"I'll happily stop asking you about it if you tell me."

"Like I said, there wasn't any motive. It was an impulsive act, done in the heat of the moment. That's all. I got angry and I killed him. There's no reason or logic to it beyond that."

"People typically don't get angry for no reason."

"Well, whatever reason I had, it wasn't anything important. To be honest, I have no idea why I lost my head. I guess that's why they call it 'losing your head.' Even if I wanted to explain it to you, I couldn't."

"Do you really think I'm going to accept that for an answer?"

"I don't think you have a choice."

I looked at him and he again met my gaze, his eyes full of self-assurance.

"I'd like to ask you again about the notebooks and disks we found in your apartment."

He looked disappointed. "Those have nothing to do with your case. Please stop trying to tie everything up into one neat little package."

"Then help me set them aside by telling me what they are."

"Nothing. Just notes and disks."

"Notes and disks containing the text to Kunihiko Hidaka's novels. Or, to be precise, text extraordinarily similar to Mr. Hidaka's work. One might even call them rough drafts."

He snorted. "What, do you think I was his ghostwriter? That's rich. You're overthinking this."

"It's the only thing that makes sense."

"How about I give you an answer that makes even more sense. Those notes you found were my homework. People who want to become writers have to work at it, you know. I practiced by copying Hidaka's works, trying to learn the rhythm of his writing, the manner of his expressions. It's nothing new or unusual. Lots of would-be authors do the same thing."

I'd been expecting him to come up with something along these lines. When I'd spoken with Kunihiko Hidaka's editor, he'd made exactly the same conjecture. However, the editor had pointed out that, even if that was the case, it still left three questions unanswered. The first was why the manuscripts we'd discovered contained slight variations from Kunihiko Hidaka's work. The second was that, although it wasn't unthinkable that someone might copy an entire novel, it certainly was unusual that someone had copied so many by the same author. The third was that, while Kunihiko Hidaka was a bestselling author, his prose wasn't so amazing that another writer would look to it as a model.

I raised these same points now to Osamu Nonoguchi himself.

Without flinching, he told me, "As for that, there are perfectly rational reasons for all of them. In the beginning, in fact, I did simply copy what Hidaka had written word for word, but eventually I got tired of that. Eventually, whenever an expression popped into my head, or a different way of saying something came to me, I would try writing that down instead. You understand? I was using Hidaka's work as a starting point, but was trying to write something better. That ultimately became the whole point of the exercise. As far as the number of novels I rewrote, well, all I can say is that I kept at it for a long time. I'm single, and there wasn't much else to do when I got home, so I wrote. It's as simple as that. As for your last point, it's true that Hidaka's writing isn't all that great, but I think you're looking at it the wrong way. His writing *is* good. It might not be the most technically advanced, but it's simple, easy to understand, and solid. I'd argue that the simple fact that so many people read it is proof enough."

Osamu Nonoguchi's explanations made sense. Yet they raised another question. Why, if all this was true, hadn't he said so earlier? Instead, he'd refused to talk about the writings we'd found at his apartment at all until now, after he collapsed in the interrogation room. I wondered if he hadn't used the break in his interrogation that resulted from his collapse and subsequent hospital stay to make up a suitable story. Of course, even if this was true, it would be exceedingly difficult to prove.

I decided to change tactics and bring up another piece of evidence we'd discovered: a collection of several memos found in Osamu Nonoguchi's desk drawer. The memos added up to the outline of a story, and the characters' names in them proved they were an outline for *The Gates of Ice*. However, it wasn't an outline of the parts already serialized. It was an outline for the remainder of the story, the part not yet written.

His explanation: "That was just more practice. Even readers like to guess where a story is going, right? I was just being a bit more hands-on about it."

"But you'd already given up your teaching career and were working as a full-time professional writer, no? Why spend so much time copying another writer's work when you could have been writing your own stories?"

"Don't be silly, I'm nowhere near what one might call a 'pro.' I still have a lot to learn. And I have plenty of time to practice, since I wasn't getting much work."

I was unconvinced.

He must've seen it in my face, because he went on, "I know you want to make me out to be Hidaka's ghostwriter, but you're giving me too much credit. I don't have that kind of talent. Besides, if it were true, I'd be shouting it from the rooftops: 'Those were all my novels! I'm the real author!' Unfortunately, I didn't write them. If I had written them, believe me, I'd have done so under my own name. Why use his? Didn't you wonder about that at all?"

"I did indeed. That's why it's all so strange."

"There's nothing strange about it. You've just made an erroneous assumption and it's leading you to strange conclusions. You're just thinking about it way too much."

"I don't think so."

"I wish you would think so, and I really don't want to talk about this anymore. Can't we just get on with the trial? Who cares about my motive? Just make up a plausible one and I'll write my confession however you please."

He sounded as though he truly *didn't* care.

I reflected on our discussion after leaving his hospital room. No matter how you looked at it, too many things didn't add up. Yet clearly, also, as he'd insisted, my reasoning had a flaw.

If he had really been Kunihiko Hidaka's ghostwriter, I had to wonder why. Had he thought the novels would sell better because Mr. Hidaka was an established author? That didn't make sense because the book that had kicked off Mr. Hidaka's career—the one that had made him a bestselling writer—was one likely written by Osamu Nonoguchi himself. He had no reason at that stage to publish it under Hidaka's name. So why not make it his own first novel?

Perhaps he'd withheld his name because he was still working as a teacher then? But that didn't make sense either. I couldn't think of an instance where a teacher had been fired for moonlighting as an author, so what would have been the purpose? And if he'd been forced to choose between professions,

I was sure that Osamu Nonoguchi would have chosen author over teacher.

Finally, as Mr. Nonoguchi himself said, if he was Mr. Hidaka's ghostwriter, why deny it? Being recognized as the true author of Kunihiko Hidaka's many works would be a feather in his cap.

So maybe he wasn't a ghostwriter. Maybe the notebooks and disks found in his apartment were nothing more than what he claimed them to be.

Except, that couldn't be true.

The Osamu Nonoguchi that I knew was prideful, confident in his abilities. I couldn't conceive of him copying so much of someone else's work, even in the attempt to become a better writer.

Back at the station, I related my discussion with Mr. Nonoguchi to the chief. Detective Sakoda listened to my report with a sour look.

When I was finished, he commented, "Why would Nonoguchi want to hide his motive for killing Hidaka?"

"I don't know. What secret could be worse than the fact that he killed someone?"

"You think Hidaka's novels are somehow involved?"

"I do."

"And that Osamu Nonoguchi was the real author? Even though he denies it?"

The department clearly didn't want to spend any more time on this case than it had to. People from the press had already started asking questions about the ghostwriter theory, though I had no idea how they'd caught wind of it. We'd avoided saying anything about it, but the papers would probably start printing stories about it, possibly even as soon as tomorrow. That would in turn mean another flood of phone calls.

"So he's claiming he just got mad and killed him?" Detective Sakoda shook his head. "That makes it sound like there was an argument, but if we don't know what that argument was about, then we don't have a place to begin. Honestly, I wouldn't mind if he just used his authorial talents to make something up. Of course, then he might contradict himself on the stand and we'd be back to square one."

"I don't believe he impulsively kill Hidaka as the result of an argument," I said. "If Osamu Nonoguchi left the house through the front door, then went around to the garden and snuck in through the window, he already had intent to kill before the deed was done. My guess is that his motive for killing him emerged during that first meeting with Hidaka."

"So the question is, what were they talking about?"

"Nonoguchi's own account of the meeting doesn't mention anything of consequence. What I think is that they were discussing how to continue their working relationship once Hidaka moved to Canada. Maybe Hidaka said something that didn't sit well with him?"

"Maybe so."

We'd already looked into Osamu Nonoguchi's bank records, but we found no indication that money was being regularly received from Kunihiko Hidaka. That didn't rule out the possibility of cash transactions, though.

"It looks like we're going to have to dig deeper into their past," the chief said.

I agreed.

. . .

I decided to pay a visit, along with two of my fellow detectives, to Rie Hidaka. She'd left the house where her husband was killed and was staying at her family home in Mitaka, a suburb in the western part of Tokyo. This was the first time I'd seen her since Osamu Nonoguchi's arrest. The chief had called ahead to break the news. He avoided mentioning the ghostwriter theory, but she'd likely heard something from the press, who were probably calling her around the clock. I imagined she had as many questions for us as we had for her.

After arriving and briefly explaining all that had happened, I told her about the manuscripts we'd found in Mr. Nonoguchi's apartment. She was surprised.

I asked her if she could think of any reason why he'd be in possession of manuscripts closely resembling her late husband's work.

She insisted she had no idea: "I don't think my husband was getting his ideas from anyone else, let alone copying someone else's work. Writing, and coming up with new ideas, was always a struggle for him, but he wasn't the type to hire a ghostwriter." Though her voice was calm, fire was in her eyes.

I had trouble believing that. She'd only been married to Kunihiko Hidaka for a month. I was sure there was much about her late husband that she didn't know.

She must have picked up on my hesitation because she went on, "If you're thinking about how long we were married— not very long, I admit—allow me to point out that before I was his wife, I was his editor."

I already knew this. Rie had worked at one of Hidaka's publishers, which was how they'd met in the first place.

"When I was his editor, we spoke at great length about the novels he might write in the future. In the end, I was the editor for only one of his books, but it's a novel that never would've existed without our discussions. I don't see how Nonoguchi could've been involved at all."

"Which novel was this?"

"*Sea Ghost*. It was published last year."

It wasn't one I'd read, so I asked one of the detectives with me if he knew anything about it. In our investigation, many of my fellow detectives had become experts on Kunihiko Hidaka's work.

His response was intriguing. *Sea Ghost* was one of the novels lacking a counterpart in Osamu Nonoguchi's notes and disks.

Nor was *Sea Ghost* alone in this. All of the novels Mr. Hidaka had published in the first three years of his career appeared to be originals. Even after that point, nearly half of his books had no counterparts in Nonoguchi's apartment. This made sense if we assumed that Mr. Hidaka continued some of his own writing, even while using Mr. Nonoguchi as a ghostwriter for other works.

If that assumption was correct, then even if there was a work that, as Rie Hidaka claimed, "never would've existed without our discussions," it didn't disprove my theory.

I tried a new angle to see if Rie had any idea what might drive Osamu Nonoguchi to kill her husband.

She said, "I've been thinking about it ever since he was arrested, but I just don't know. To be honest, I still can't believe he did it. They were such good friends. I don't think I ever saw them fight or argue. I worry that this might all be some horrible mistake."

I believe she was sincere. Nothing in her manner suggested this was just a performance for our benefit. I asked a few minor follow-up questions, then I thanked her for her time.

As we were getting ready to leave, Rie Hidaka handed me a book with a gray jacket, speckled as though with gold dust—a copy of *Sea Ghost*. I think what she had in mind was that I read it and then stop doubting her late husband's talent.

I began reading it that night, recalling that Osamu Nonoguchi had recommended this very book to me when I asked him if Kunihiko Hidaka had ever written a mystery. I wondered if there was a deeper meaning behind Nonoguchi's choice of book. Was he suggesting I read a Hidaka novel that he had nothing to do with?

Sea Ghost was the story of a man of advanced years and his young wife. The man was a painter, the wife his model. The painter began to suspect that his wife was cheating on him, a typical theme for the genre. However, the wife had two distinct personalities, and the real action kicks off when the husband discovers her secret. One of her personalities is his loyal wife who seems to love him from the bottom of her heart. The other personality has a lover, and it becomes clear this personality is plotting with her lover to kill the painter. As the painter agonizes over whether he should bring her to a hospital for treatment, he finds a memo on his desk:

"Who will the drugs kill? Me? Or her?"

The memo had been left by his wife's "other" personality, and the message was clear: even if treatment could fix her multiple-personality disorder, there was no guarantee that the personality who loved him would be the one that remained.

Deeply troubled, the painter begins having nightmares. In these dreams, his wife comes into the room with an angelic smile on her face and opens the bedroom window, through which a man enters. As the intruder lifts a knife to attack the painter, the intruder's face changes to become that of the wife—at which point the painter wakes in a cold sweat.

In the end, a real attempt is made on his life, and defending himself, the painter accidentally stabs his wife. She dies in his arms, but the way she looks at him makes him believe that, just before the end, her personality shifted back to that of the good wife. So, did he kill the angel or the demon? The painter is doomed never to know.

That's the general outline, though I'm sure a more discerning reader might have come away with a higher-level interpretation. Themes such as lust in old age, and ugliness in the heart of an artist, were probably there for the taking if one read between the lines, but I was never much for literature in school. Nor am I particularly qualified to pass judgment on the quality of the writing itself. That said, with all due respect to Rie Hidaka, in my opinion it wasn't a very good book.

Let's consider the careers of the two men: killer and victim.

Kunihiko Hidaka joined a private high school attached to a university and climbed up that ladder into the university's Department of Literature and Philosophy. After getting a degree, he worked first at an advertising company, then at a publisher. Roughly ten years ago, a short story he'd written won a small literary magazine's new-author award. This started his career as a novelist. For the next two years, none of his books sold all that well, but the book he published in the fourth year, *An Unburning Flame,* won a major award for literature. This began his march toward being a famous author.

Osamu Nonoguchi went to a different private high school from Hidaka's and, after taking a year off, began studying in the literature department of a national university. His major was in Japanese literature. He got his teaching credentials and after graduation took a job at a public middle school. He worked at three schools before he retired from teaching earlier this year. The school where we worked together was the second of those three.

Nonoguchi made his own authorial debut three years ago with a short story published in a biannual children's magazine. To date, he hasn't yet published a novel.

Though they took different paths, according to Osamu Nonoguchi, the two met again about seven years ago. He claims to have seen Hidaka's name in a newspaper and reached out to reconnect with his old friend.

I believe this is the truth because roughly half a year after they supposedly reconnected, Hidaka won the literature prize for *An Unburning Flame,* which is the first of his books with a version found in Nonoguchi's manuscripts. It seems safe to assume that Hidaka's reunion with Nonoguchi brought a change in his fortunes.

I went to speak to the editor of *An Unburning Flame.* A short fellow by the name of Mimura, he was currently serving as the chief editor of a literary magazine.

I asked him if he could imagine Kunihiko Hidaka writing *An Unburning Flame* based on what he had written before.

Before he answered my question, Mr. Mimura had one of his own: "Are you investigating that ridiculous ghostwriter theory that's been making the rounds?"

Clearly, Mr. Mimura wasn't a fan of my theory. Nor did his company have anything to gain by besmirching Kunihiko Hidaka's work, even after his death.

"I wouldn't call it a theory, there's not enough evidence to call it that. I just need to make sure we have all the facts straight."

"Well, it seems like a waste of time to follow up on baseless rumors, but you don't need me to tell you how to do your job." Then he answered my question: "When you get right down to it, *An Unburning Flame* was a turning point for Mr. Hidaka. He showed tremendous growth as a writer in that novel. Some might say he transformed overnight."

"Would you say it was considerably better than what he had written before?"

"It was, but for me—and this is critical—it wasn't all that unexpected. Hidaka was always a powerful writer. But his earlier work was always a little too rough at the edges, and he lost readers because of it. They couldn't grasp the message through the noise, if you follow. However, *An Unburning Flame* was very streamlined. Have you read it?"

"I did. It was good."

"I agree. In fact, I think it's his best work."

It was the story of a salaryman who, enchanted by the beauty of the fireworks he sees while on a business trip, changes professions and becomes a fireworks maker. The story was good, but the descriptions of the fireworks in particular were well done, I thought.

"And he wrote that novel all in one go. It wasn't serialized?"

"That's correct."

"Did you talk about the work before he started writing it?"

"Of course. We do that with every author."

"What did you talk about with Mr. Hidaka at that time?"

"We discussed the plot a little. We also talked theme, story, and his main character."

"Did you make all of the big decisions together, then?"

"No. Naturally that's left to Mr. Hidaka to do by himself. He's the author, after all. I just help him talk through his ideas and offer my opinions."

"Was it Mr. Hidaka's idea to have the main character become a fireworks maker?"

"Of course."

"What did you think when you heard that?"

"You mean did I like it?"

"Did it seem like his kind of idea?"

"Not particularly, but it certainly wasn't a surprise, either. He's not the first person to write about fireworks makers."

"Would you say that there was anything in the final book that was the direct result of your advice, Mr. Mimura?"

"Nothing big. I looked at the finished manuscript and pointed out a few things, sure, but it was up to him to decide how to fix them."

"One last question. If Mr. Hidaka had rewritten someone else's work using his own words and expressions, do you think you could tell by reading it?"

Mr. Mimura thought a while before answering, "Honestly, no. Word usage and turns of phrase are the best way to tell who the writer is, so, no, I suppose not."

But he didn't neglect to add, "Detective, *An Unburning Flame* is without a doubt Mr. Hidaka's work. We met several times during its writing, and he was truly struggling with it. Sometimes I thought he might have a breakdown altogether. If he was using someone else's novel as a basis, I doubt he would have had to struggle quite so much."

I refrained from venturing an opinion on this and instead thanked him and left. However, I had already worked out a rebuttal in my mind. Namely, that while it was difficult when times were hard to pretend to be happy, doing the reverse was relatively simple. Nothing he'd said shook my confidence in my ghostwriter theory.

When one man kills another, often a woman is involved. However, we hadn't yet looked deeply into the possibility of there being a woman in Osamu Nonoguchi's life. The feeling in the department was that it wasn't one of "those kind of murders." Or maybe it was just the impression we had of Mr. Nonoguchi himself. He wasn't unattractive, but it was hard to picture the woman who would choose him.

However, our instincts were wrong. He had had a special relationship with at least one woman. The investigation team that performed the follow-up search of his apartment found the first evidence of this, three clues.

The first was an apron with a checkered pattern and a feminine design, found neatly ironed and folded in one of Osamu Nonoguchi's dressers. Our working theory is that a woman who occasionally visited would wear it when she cleaned up around the apartment or perhaps cooked meals.

The second clue was a gold necklace, still in its case, and

neatly wrapped. The necklace came from a famous jewelry store. It looked like a present waiting to be given.

The third clue was a filled-out questionnaire, folded neatly and placed in the same box as the wrapped necklace. The questionnaire came from a travel agency and concerned a trip to Okinawa Mr. Nonoguchi had apparently been planning. The date at the top of the questionnaire was May 10, seven years ago. The trip was planned for July 30, neatly coinciding with a teacher's summer break. However, since the questionnaire had never been turned in, it seemed that the trip never happened.

At issue were the names of the travelers: Osamu Nonoguchi, and right next to that, a Hatsuko Nonoguchi, age twenty-nine.

We looked into it, and no one with that name ever existed. At least, not among Osamu Nonoguchi's relatives. Our assumption is that Hatsuko Nonoguchi was an alias, and Osamu was intending to take a trip to Okinawa with a woman pretending to be his wife.

From this we can assume the following: at the very least, seven years ago, Osamu Nonoguchi was in a close relationship with a woman, and though the current status of that relationship was unknown, he still had feelings for her—enough that he kept the relics of their relationship close at hand.

I asked the chief for permission to investigate further. I had no idea whether Hatsuko was connected to our case; however, seven years ago was the year before Kunihiko Hidaka broke out with *An Unburning Flame*. I felt that, were I able to meet the woman Nonoguchi was with at the time, I might learn something of value about what was going on then.

I first tried asking the man himself. He sat up halfway in his hospital bed when I told him we'd found the apron, the necklace, and the travel documents.

"Could you please tell us whom the apron belongs to, to whom you intended to give the necklace, and with whom you were planning on going to Okinawa?"

Unlike my previous questions, these clearly troubled him. "What does that have to do with your case? I realize I'm a murderer, and I have to pay for my crimes, but does that mean I have to divulge private matters that have nothing to do with my crime?"

"I'm not telling you to make it public knowledge. You only have to tell me. If we find that this has nothing to do with the murder, I won't ask you about it again, nor will the media hear about it. I can guarantee that we won't bother the woman."

"Well, I'm sorry, but she has nothing to do with the case. You'll have to trust me on that."

"Then why don't you just tell me? If you refuse, you'll be forcing us to investigate, and I guarantee you that we'll find out everything there is to know. Once our detectives start looking at this, there's a good chance that the press will catch wind of it. I imagine that's not something you particularly want."

But no matter what I said, Osamu Nonoguchi wouldn't tell us the woman's name. He even took issue with our continuing to search his apartment: "I'd prefer you stopped rooting through my things. Some of my books were gifts from friends, and they're very important to me."

At that point, however, the doctor intervened. I'd reach the time limit he'd placed on my visit and I was forced to leave.

I felt I had achieved what I needed that day, for I was now convinced that looking for this mysterious woman would be a meaningful step in establishing Nonoguchi's motive.

I began by speaking with Mr. Nonoguchi's neighbors, asking if they'd seen a woman in his apartment or heard a woman's voice there. People who are normally reluctant to answer most questions from the police frequently become overly eager to help when it comes to their neighbor's relationships. In this case, however, my questions didn't yield much. Even the woman who lived next door to Nonoguchi, a housewife who was often home, said she'd never seen a woman visit his apartment.

"It doesn't have to be recently. In fact, it might have been several years since she last visited."

The neighbor told me she had been living there almost ten years, meaning she'd moved in around the same time as Nonoguchi. It seemed likely she'd have seen anyone he was dating.

"Maybe there was a woman," she said at last. "But that was some time ago, and I'm afraid I just don't remember."

I tried taking a fresh look at all of Osamu Nonoguchi's relationships—personal and professional. I started by visiting the middle school he'd quit back in March. However, I found that few people there knew anything at all about his personal life. He'd never been much for socializing, and he'd never spent time with anyone from the school outside of work.

I next went to the middle school where he'd taught before that. This was where he was working when the Okinawa trip was planned. I wasn't eager about visiting that school because this was where I'd once taught as well.

I waited for classes to finish before going. Two of the three school buildings had been renovated, but that was about the only difference. Everything else looked exactly as it had ten years before.

Suddenly lacking the courage to walk through the front gate, I stood there and watched the students leave school. Then a familiar face passed in front of me, an English teacher named Mrs. Tone. She was about seven or eight years older than me. I went after her and called out to her. She turned, recognizing me with a surprised smile.

I said hello and asked how she was before telling her that I wanted to talk about Nonoguchi. She nodded, her expression growing serious.

We went to a nearby coffee shop, a place that had opened since I'd worked at the school.

"We were all surprised by what happened, and no one can believe that Mr. Nonoguchi was the killer," she told me, then added excitedly, "And to think that you're on the case! What a coincidence."

I told her that this coincidence was making it hard for me to do my job, which she said she understood. Then I got down to the matter at hand. My first question was whether there ever was a woman in Osamu Nonoguchi's life.

She said it was a difficult question. "I don't know for sure, but my feeling is there wasn't."

"What makes you say that?"

"Intuition?" She laughed. "I know, I know. 'Intuition' is usually dead wrong. But . . . I think some objective facts make this likely the case. Did you know that Mr. Nonoguchi had a bunch of people set him up on blind dates?"

"No, I didn't. He doesn't strike me as the dating type."

"It was less random dating and more like he was looking for a potential spouse. I'm pretty sure our headmaster at the time set him up at least once. If he was so desperate to get hitched, I can't imagine there was a woman in his life."

"How many years ago are we talking?"

"It wasn't that long before he left the school, so maybe five or six years ago?"

"What about before then? Was he getting set up then, too?"

"I don't remember exactly. Should I ask some of the other teachers? There are still quite a few who were here in those days."

I told her that would be a huge help if she would check around with her colleagues.

Mrs. Tone pulled out a PDA and wrote herself a memo.

I moved on to my second question, asking if she knew anything about Osamu Nonoguchi's relationship with Kuni-hiko Hidaka.

"Oh, that's right," she said, "you'd already left the school by then."

"By when?"

"By the time Kunihiko Hidaka won that new-author award."

"I'm not sure if I was here or not. I'm not the sort who keeps tabs on literature awards."

"Oh, I wouldn't have known about it myself if Mr. Nono-guchi hadn't brought the announcement to school and showed it to everyone. He seemed very excited that his old schoolmate had won."

"Do you know if Mr. Nonoguchi was in contact with Mr. Hidaka at that time?"

"I'm not sure, but I don't think so, not at that point. He did eventually meet up with him, I know, but that was some time after that."

"How long after? Could it have been two or three years?" That would mean his reunion with Hidaka was seven years ago, as he'd claimed.

"Sure, that sounds about right."

"Did Mr. Nonoguchi ever talk about Mr. Hidaka in detail?"

"What kind of detail?"

"Anything at all. Maybe he commented on what kind of person his old friend was, or maybe he said something about his novels."

"I don't remember if he said anything about Mr. Hidaka as a person, but he was a little outspoken about not liking his writing very much."

"He didn't think his novels were good? Do you remember anything specific?"

"Oh, he would always say more or less the same things. That Mr. Hidaka didn't understand literature, or he couldn't write people, or that his books were too lowbrow."

This sounded nothing like what I'd heard about Hidaka's writing from Osamu Nonoguchi. Nor like the words of someone who had held up Hidaka's books as a model for his own writing.

"But he still read Hidaka's books even though he didn't like them? And he went to visit him?"

"He did. Honestly, I think he only said those negative things about Mr. Hidaka's work because of his own mixed feelings."

"What do you mean?"

"Well, you see, Mr. Nonoguchi always wanted to be a writer, and his childhood friend beat him to it. But he couldn't just ignore what his friend was doing. Of course he thought, 'What's so great about these? I could write better.'"

Now that, I could picture.

"Do you remember how Mr. Nonoguchi reacted when Kunihiko Hidaka won the award for *An Unburning Flame?*"

"Well, it'd make a better story if he'd been wracked with jealousy, but actually, I don't think he was. In fact, he sounded pretty proud of it."

I could interpret this a number of ways, but it was good information. Though I wasn't able to find out anything about a girlfriend, I wasn't leaving empty-handed. I thanked Mrs. Tone for her time.

That business behind us, Mrs. Tone asked me how I'd been since I left teaching, and how my new job was going. I said something harmless, mostly avoided talking about my departure from the school, which wasn't my favorite topic.

I believe she understood this and she didn't press too hard. Except at the end when she said, "You know, bullying is still a problem."

"I don't doubt it." I had spent years noticing every time bullying was mentioned in the news. Mostly because the guilt over my own failure hadn't ever left me.

We left the coffee shop, and Mrs. Tone and I parted ways.

•   •   •

The photograph turned up the day after my meeting with
Mrs. Tone. Makimura discovered it during yet another search
of the Nonoguchi apartment.

We'd come back again hoping to find a little more information on the woman, Hatsuko. Our main goal was to find a
photo. I was certain that someone who so carefully stored mementos such as the apron was sure to have a photo around
somewhere, yet none had turned up. There were some albums,
but none of the photos in them were of women of the right age.
This seemed odd.

"Why wouldn't Nonoguchi keep a photo?" I asked Makimura during a break.

"Maybe he didn't have one? People usually take couples
shots if they go somewhere together, but assuming they never
made it to Okinawa, maybe the opportunity never presented
itself?"

"Really? This is a man who kept old travel documents in
his dresser. Surely he would've taken at least one photo."

The apron suggested that the woman had come to the
apartment regularly. We knew he owned a camera and could've
taken a picture of her during one of her visits.

"Well," Makimura said, "if there was a photo and we
haven't found it, it's because he's hidden it."

"Exactly what I was thinking. But why hide it? He certainly wasn't expecting a police search."

"Another mystery."

I was looking around the room again when something
Mr. Nonoguchi said to me the other day popped into my head,
something about his not wanting us to root through his things
anymore—his books, in particular.

A bookshelf ran the length of his office wall. I divided the books up between myself and Detective Makimura, and we searched each one, cover to cover, checking for any photos, letters, or notes stuck between the pages.

This took over two hours. As one might expect of a writer, he owned a large number of books. As we searched, the piles towered around us like miniature Leaning Towers of Pisa.

Eventually it occurred to me that I might have gotten it wrong. Why keep a photograph if it was so well hidden you couldn't take it out to look at it? It made more sense for him to have it in a place where he could easily grab it and quickly put it away again.

Makimura went to the table with Mr. Nonoguchi's word processor on it. He sat down, pretending to be the author at work. "So, I'm working on my latest masterpiece, and my thoughts drift to her. I suppose he could put a photo right around here." Makimura indicated the blank space directly next to the word processor.

"What about a place you can't see, but is always within reach?"

Detective Makimura looked around, spotting a thick dictionary with gaps in between pages where Nonoguchi had left bookmarks. He smiled and reached for it. His guess was on the mark. Five bookmarks were inside the dictionary, one of them a photo of a young woman standing in front of what appeared to be a roadside restaurant. She was wearing a checkered blouse and a white skirt.

It didn't take long to find out who she was. Rie Hidaka identified her immediately. She was Hatsumi Hidaka—Kunihiko Hidaka's late wife.

"Hatsumi's maiden name was Shinoda," she told us. "They were married for twelve years, which lasted until she died in a traffic accident five years ago now. I never met her. She'd already passed away when I met Hidaka. But I knew her face from the albums he still had at home. That's definitely her."

I asked if we could see those albums, but she shook her head. "I don't have them anymore. Right after we got married, he sent them and everything else of hers back to her family. There might be something left in the stuff we sent to Canada, but I'm not sure. I'll take a look though. Our things are being returned and they are supposed to arrive back in Japan any day now."

I asked if she thought he'd sent the albums back to the family out of respect for her.

Rie frowned. "Perhaps he was doing it for my sake, but I honestly didn't mind having her things there. After all, they were married a long time. I thought it would be only natural if he'd wanted to have some keepsakes of her around. But he didn't keep anything and he never once spoke about her to me. Maybe it was too painful for him? For my part, I never brought it up. It wasn't out of jealousy or anything, there just never was a need."

It seemed to me that Rie was going out of her way not to sound too emotional, though nothing in what she said struck me as unusual or suspicious. Incidentally, she did appear curious as to why we had a photo of her husband's late wife. She asked whether it had anything to do with the case.

"We're not sure yet," I told her, then added vaguely, "The

photo came from a rather unexpected place, so we thought we should look into it."

"What do you mean an 'unexpected place'?"

I regretted saying it immediately. "I'm sorry, but I can't say any more at this time."

However, her intuition was already working overtime. A shocked look came over her face. "You know, I think it was at my husband's wake, but Mr. Nonoguchi recently asked me a strange question."

"What's that?"

"He wanted to know where our videotapes were."

"Videotapes?"

"I thought he was talking about the movies my husband had been collecting. Except it wasn't that. He was asking about the videos Hidaka took for research."

"You mean, your husband took videos when he was doing research for a novel?"

"Yes, particularly when the subject he was researching was something living, or moving, he would bring a video camera along with him on his research trips."

"What did you tell Mr. Nonoguchi?"

"I told him I thought the tapes had been sent on to Canada. When we were having the house packed up, my husband handled all of his work-related things, so I honestly wasn't sure."

"What did Nonoguchi say to that?"

"He asked me to tell him when our things were returned from Canada. He said he'd loaned some tapes that he'd used in his own work to Hidaka, and they were probably mixed in with Hidaka's."

"He didn't say what the tapes contained?"

Rie shook her head, then looked back at me. "You think maybe she's on one of the tapes?"

She meant Hatsumi Hidaka. I didn't comment on that, but I did ask her to let us know when the tapes arrived back from Canada.

Then I asked a final question, not really expecting an answer. "Did Mr. Nonoguchi say anything else to you that struck you as odd?"

She hesitated at first, but then said, "It wasn't at the funeral, it was a few months ago. Mr. Nonoguchi mentioned Hatsumi just once."

"In what context?"

"It was about the accident."

"Oh? What did he say about it?"

Rie hesitated again, then it seemed she'd made up her mind. "He said he didn't think it was just an accident."

That was quite a statement. I asked her to elaborate.

"That's the thing, he didn't say any more than that. This happened when he was over at our house and my husband had left the room for a moment. I don't even remember how it came up, but I couldn't forget those words."

I didn't blame her. It was quite the thing to say to a man's fiancée.

"If it wasn't 'just an accident,' what was it? What did you say to him?"

"Well, I asked what he meant. Then he looked like he regretted having said anything and told me to forget about it and not mention it to my husband."

"And did you talk to your husband about it?"

"Actually, I didn't. Like I said, we didn't talk about his late wife in the first place, and that certainly wasn't the kind of thing one could lightly mention."

On this point, I had to agree.

Just to be sure, we showed the photograph to other people who knew Hatsumi Hidaka well: editors that used to visit Hidaka's house, and people in the neighborhood. Everyone confirmed that she was the woman in the photograph.

The only question remaining was, why did Osamu Nonoguchi keep a photograph of Hatsumi Hidaka hidden on his desk?

There didn't seem to be much room for interpretation here. The woman who owned the apron found in his apartment, the intended recipient of the necklace, the would-be traveling companion to Okinawa, had been Hidaka's late wife. It wasn't too much of a stretch to imagine that *Hatsuko* was an alias for *Hatsumi*. She had been married to Hidaka, which meant that her relationship with Nonoguchi was an extramarital affair. If this was true, the relationship had to have developed during the two years between Osamu Nonoguchi's reunion with Kunihiko Hidaka seven years ago and Hatsumi Hidaka's death.

I grew increasingly convinced that this relationship was related to Nonoguchi's motive for killing Hidaka. Let me return to my theory that Osamu Nonoguchi was working as Kunihiko Hidaka's ghostwriter. All the evidence clearly points to this except, once again, Nonoguchi's motive is unclear. There was no sign of any monetary arrangement—no paperwork or evidence of money changing hands. Furthermore, after speaking with several editors on the topic, it appeared that writers just aren't inclined to sell off their work without any recognition—especially not work that might earn them critical acclaim.

But what if Nonoguchi owed Hidaka some immense debt?

This is where, I believe, Hatsumi Hidaka comes into the picture. It's not a big stretch to think that Kunihiko Hidaka had caught on to the relationship and was forcing Nonoguchi to write for him in exchange for his silence. But that wouldn't explain why Nonoguchi continued to write for Hidaka even after Hatsumi's death.

Clearly, the answer was to be found by looking deeper into what had happened between Osamu Nonoguchi and the Hidakas. This would be a lot easier to do if two of the three people involved weren't already dead.

And then there was what Rie said about Nonoguchi's confiding to her that Hatsumi's death hadn't been a simple accident. Why say that to her? And if it wasn't an accident, what was it?

I decided to look more closely at the events surrounding Hatsumi's death. A check of the database showed that Hatsumi Hidaka had died in March, five years ago. She had been on her way to buy something at a nearby convenience store at eleven o'clock at night when she was hit by a truck. The accident occurred where the road had a sharp curve with poor visibility, it was raining, and there was no crosswalk.

The opinion of the judge who heard the case was that the truck driver was guilty of negligence for not paying enough attention to the road, a typical judgment in accidents involving a car and a pedestrian. Yet according to the record, the driver never admitted wrongdoing. He said that she jumped out into the road suddenly. With traffic accidents when drivers hit pedestrians, the drivers nearly always blame it on the pedestrian. Traffic cops hear that same story time and time again. In this case, if it was true, then unfortunately for the driver there were no other witnesses.

I decided to pretend that what the driver had said was accurate. If, as Osamu Nonoguchi had hinted, it wasn't a simple accident, that left two other possibilities: murder or suicide.

Murder would have to mean someone pushed her, which would place her killer at the scene. Yet someone in a position to push her far enough into the road to be hit would surely have been visible to the driver, making it unlikely that he hadn't mentioned that person in his testimony.

The logical assumption was that Osamu Nonoguchi thought Hatsumi Hidaka had committed suicide by throwing herself in front of that truck.

Why would he think that? Was there any physical evidence? Had she sent him a farewell letter? Or did Osamu Nonoguchi know of a reason Hatsumi Hidaka would have wanted to kill herself? Perhaps their affair was such a reason.

Possibly her husband had discovered her infidelity. Had she decided to kill herself because he was going to abandon her? If that was the case, then what she'd had with Nonoguchi was nothing more than a passing dalliance.

Either way, I needed to know more about Hatsumi Hidaka.

With the chief's permission, I took Detective Makimura with me to visit her family. The Shinodas lived in Yokohama's Kanazawa Ward, in a traditional house with a well-kept garden, high up on a hillside.

I'd heard both of her parents were alive and well, but her father was out that day, so we met with her mother, Yumie Shinoda, a diminutive, well-dressed lady.

She didn't seem terribly surprised by our visit. To the contrary, she wondered why we hadn't come earlier. Apparently, she'd been expecting us ever since she'd heard Kunihiko Hidaka had been killed.

We asked her for her impression of her son-in-law.

"Oh, he had a difficult temperament, like anyone else in his profession. Hatsumi told me once that he could get on your nerves when he was having trouble with his work. Yet I think he was a good husband most of the time. A very thoughtful man."

It was difficult for me to tell whether she was being honest or just saying something safe. It's always hardest to tell what older people, particularly women, are really thinking.

According to her, Kunihiko Hidaka and her daughter had met when they were both working at a small ad agency. While they were dating, Hidaka had moved to a job at a publishing company, and they had gotten married shortly thereafter. Not long after that he won the new-author award and left his job in publishing to become a full-time writer.

"My husband and I were a little worried about giving our daughter away to someone who changed professions so frequently, yet they never seemed to have money trouble. Of course once Kunihiko became a bestselling author, we were very happy and knew we wouldn't have to worry about our daughter being provided for. Then the accident . . . I'm afraid all the money in the world can't help you after something like that."

Though Mrs. Shinoda's eyes teared up, she didn't cry in

front of us. I believe she'd had time in the intervening five years to make peace with what had happened.

"I understand that the accident occurred while she was on the way to the store?" I asked.

"That's what Kunihiko said. She'd gone to buy bread to make a midnight sandwich."

"The truck driver claims that she jumped suddenly out onto the road."

"So I heard. But she wasn't the kind to do anything so reckless! That spot she tried to cross, that's a bad spot. The visibility is poor and she was probably hurrying too."

"Do you know how the Hidakas were doing as a couple prior to the accident?"

Mrs. Shinoda seemed surprised by the question. "They were fine. Why do you ask?"

"No reason in particular. Just that many people who get into accidents have worries on their mind and aren't paying attention to their surroundings," I explained quickly.

"As far as I remember, everything was going well. Kunihiko had just started a new novel, so she was a little lonely."

"She told you this?" I wondered if that loneliness might not be the key. "Did you see her much before the accident?"

"No. Her husband was busy with his work, and she didn't come back here very often. We would talk on the phone now and then, though."

"Did you sense anything different about her voice, anything at all?"

The old woman shook her head, then hesitated before saying, "Is there some connection between my daughter and what happened to Kunihiko?"

I told her no, probably not, and explained that when there's
been a murder, it is a detective's duty to look into everyone
the victim or the perpetrator knew, even those who'd passed
away. I'm not sure she entirely bought my explanation.

"Did your daughter ever talk to you about Osamu Nonoguchi?" I said, bringing the discussion around to the key point.

"I heard that he sometimes visited. He was a friend of
Kunihiko's who wanted to be an author?"

"Anything else?"

"Well, it was a long while ago, and I don't remember things
as clearly as I used to. But I don't think she talked about him
that much."

It occurred to me that, especially if they were having an affair, the last person she would mention him to was her mother.

"I heard that most of her personal belongings were sent
back here. Would it be possible for us to have a look?"

Hatsumi's mother seemed taken aback. "We don't have
much."

"Anything would be helpful."

"Well, I don't see how . . ."

"Did she keep a diary by any chance?"

"No, nothing of that sort."

"Any photo albums?"

"Well, yes . . ."

"Could we see those, please?"

"They are just filled with pictures of Kunihiko and
Hatsumi."

"That's more than enough. We'll be able to tell quickly if
there's anything helpful in there."

She must have wondered what I was talking about. I

knew things would go more quickly if I mentioned her daughter's potential connection to Osamu Nonoguchi, but the chief hadn't given me permission to mention that yet.

Though she still seemed suspicious, she went into the back and brought out some albums. These simple things, plastic folders with sleeved pages, were all stuffed into a box.

Detective Makimura and I looked through each one. The woman in them was without a doubt the same one in the photo from Osamu Nonoguchi's apartment.

Since most of the photos had a date stamp, it wasn't difficult to find ones from the time when she was supposedly in contact with Nonoguchi. I looked at these carefully, trying to find some hint that might suggest a connection.

Again, Makimura found the photo we were looking for. He handed it to me in silence. I understood immediately why he had picked it out.

I asked Yumie Shinoda if we could borrow that album for a while. She gave me a dubious look but agreed.

"Do you have anything else of Hatsumi's around?"

"Just some jewelry and clothing. I don't think Kunihiko wanted her things around the house, since he was getting remarried."

"Nothing written? Letters or postcards?"

"I don't think so. I can take a closer look."

"How about videotapes? Small ones, about the size of a cassette tape?" Hidaka had used 8 mm tapes when he did his research.

"I don't think I saw anything like that, no."

"Could you tell us the names of anyone who was close to Hatsumi, then?"

"People close to her?" She frowned, thinking for a moment, then excused herself and went into a back room. When she reappeared, she was carrying a thin notebook.

"This is our address book—it has the names of some of her friends."

She picked three names out of the book. Two were classmates from her school, and one was a colleague from the advertising agency. All three were women. I took down their names and contact information.

We started contacting Ms. Hidaka's friends as soon as we got back to the office. The two from school hadn't seen her much after she got married. However, her friend from work, a woman by the name of Shizuko Nagano, had remained close, even talking to her on the phone only a few days before she died.

She told us, "I don't think Hatsumi noticed Mr. Hidaka much at first. But he came on to her pretty strong, and eventually she got sucked in—you know how it goes. Mr. Hidaka wasn't the kind to take no for an answer, either at work or in his personal life, and Hatsumi was always a little shy. She wasn't someone who wore her emotions on her sleeve. If you ask me, I think she had second thoughts when he proposed, but in the end, Mr. Hidaka won out.

"Not that she wasn't happy. She seemed like she was doing well, though maybe a little on the tired side after Mr. Hidaka became an author. Having your whole routine tossed in the air can do that. Still, I never heard her complain."

Regarding the phone call just before the accident: "I was the one who called her, though I didn't have anything in particular to talk about. She was the same as always, I'd say. I don't remember the details of our conversation, but I think we talked about restaurants and places to go shopping. That's pretty much all we ever talked about. I was really surprised when I heard about the accident. I mean, I couldn't even cry it was such a shock. I was there for the wake and the funeral."

Regarding Mr. Hidaka's bearing at the funeral: "Guys like that tend not to show much emotion in public, but it was clear to everyone he was despondent. I can't believe that was five years ago."

Regarding Osamu Nonoguchi: "Who? Was that Hidaka's killer? I don't remember whether he came to the funeral or not. There were a lot of people there. Why are the police asking about Hatsumi now, anyway? Does it have something to do with the murder?"

Two days after we visited Hatsumi Hidaka's family home, Detective Makimura and I went to see Osamu Nonoguchi in the hospital. We spoke first to his doctor.

The doctor was troubled. He was ready to perform the surgery, but the patient wouldn't give consent. Apparently, Nonoguchi was saying that, if his chances were slim anyway, he might as well skip the operation and live a little longer.

"Would the surgery hasten his death?" I asked the surgeon.

He told me it was certainly possible. However, the potential for a good outcome was enough that he felt strongly they should undertake it anyway.

With that in mind, we went to Nonoguchi's room, where we found him sitting up in bed, reading a book. He looked thin, but his complexion was good.

"I was wondering what was up. Haven't seen you around

in a while." Though he sounded well enough, his voice lacked spirit.

"I have another request," I said.

Osamu Nonoguchi looked a little disappointed. "You are unusually persistent. Or does that happen to everyone when they become a detective?"

I didn't respond, instead showing him the photo of Hatsumi Hidaka we'd found in his dictionary.

Osamu Nonoguchi's face froze, his mouth twisted slightly askew. I could hear his breathing become labored.

"Yes?" he croaked at last. I got the distinct impression that saying just that one word was all he could manage.

"Why were you in possession of a photograph of Kunihiko Hidaka's former wife? And why keep it in such an unusual place?"

Osamu Nonoguchi looked out the window, thinking. I stared hard at his face in profile.

"So what if I had a photo of Hatsumi?" he said at length, still gazing out the window. "It's got nothing to do with your case, Detective."

"Again, that's for us to decide."

"I'm telling you the truth."

"Then please explain this photograph."

"It's nothing. It doesn't mean anything. I took a photo of her at some point and forgot to give it to Hidaka."

"And used it as a bookmark?"

"It must have been lying around. I don't know."

"When was this picture taken? And where? It looks like a roadside restaurant."

"I forget. I occasionally went out with the two of them—

cherry-blossom viewing, or to see some festival. It was probably one of those trips."

"But the picture only shows her. I think it's a little odd to
go on a trip with a couple and only take a picture of the wife."

"It was a restaurant, maybe Hidaka was in the bathroom
when I took it."

"Do you have any other pictures from that trip?"

"How can I tell you that if I don't know when it was
taken? They might be in an album, or I might've thrown them
away by mistake. Either way, I don't remember."

Osamu Nonoguchi's distress was obvious.

I pulled out two more photos and placed them in front of
him. Both prominently featured Mount Fuji. "You remember
these, don't you?"

He looked at the photographs, and I caught him swal-
lowing.

"We found them in your photo album. I'm sure you haven't
forgotten these."

He shook his head. "I wonder when those were taken,"
he said, his voice weak.

"Both were taken in the same place. You don't remember
where?"

"Sorry."

"Fuji River. To be precise, the Fuji River highway rest
area. The same place as the other photo we just showed you.
Notice the staircase in the back—it's the same one."

Osamu Nonoguchi was silent.

Several of the investigators on my team had recognized the
rest area from the photo of Hatsumi. Armed with that knowledge, and with the help of the police department in Shizuoka

Prefecture, where the rest area was located, we identified two other photos taken there.

"If you can't remember when you took the photo of Hatsumi, perhaps you can tell me about these photos you took of Mount Fuji? Why is it that they were in your album, but Hatsumi's photo wasn't?"

"Sorry, I didn't even remember I had those." Apparently he had made up his mind to play dumb to the very last.

"I have one last photograph." I pulled a single photo out of my jacket pocket. This was the photo we'd borrowed from Hatsumi's mother. "Something in this one must look very familiar to you."

I watched him as he looked at the photo, which was a picture of three women standing together. It was slight, but I saw his eyes widen.

"Well?"

"I'm sorry. I have no idea what you're getting at." His voice was hoarse.

"Really? You recognize the woman in the middle, though, don't you? Hatsumi Hidaka?"

I took Nonoguchi's silence as a yes.

"How about the apron she's wearing? The yellow-and-white-checkered pattern? It's the same as the one that we found in your apartment."

"So what?"

"So you can try to explain away keeping a photo of Hatsumi however you like, but how do you intend to explain her apron being in your possession? Did you or did you not have a relationship with Hatsumi Hidaka?"

Osamu Nonoguchi moaned softly.

"Please, tell us the truth. I've said this before, but the more you hide from us, the deeper we have to dig. It's only a matter of time before the press catches on and somebody writes an article filled with conjectures. I guarantee that is something that you wouldn't want to see in print. Tell us everything now, and we can help prevent that."

I wasn't sure how much of an effect my words had made on him. The only thing I could pick up from Nonoguchi's expression was painful indecision.

At last he said, "What happened between me and Hatsumi has nothing to do with this. I want to be clear about that."

Finally, we were getting somewhere. "So you do admit to having a relationship with her?"

"I wouldn't call it a relationship. It was just a moment when our feelings might have moved toward each other. But it faded quickly, for both of us."

"When did this start?"

"I don't remember exactly. Maybe five or six months after I started visiting Hidaka. I caught a bad cold and was bedridden for a while, and she came to check on me every now and then. That's how it started."

"How long did it last?"

"Two, three months? Like I said, it wasn't long before the heat went out of it entirely. We just went crazy for a little while, that's all. It happens."

"But you continued seeing the Hidakas after that. Most people would stay away after something like that happened."

"It's not like we parted on bad terms. We talked about it and agreed we should stop seeing each other. I can't say that we entirely succeeded, that there wasn't a meaningful glance or two when I would visit. But for the most part whenever I dropped in, she would be out. I think she was avoiding it. Avoiding us. I believe that if she hadn't had that accident, I would have stopped seeing either of them before long."

Once he got going, Osamu Nonoguchi spoke easily, the fear and hesitation he'd shown moments before now gone. I watched his expression, trying to determine how much of this I could believe. Though there were no telltale signs that he was lying, it was strange that he was suddenly so calm.

"In addition to the apron, we found a necklace and travel documents."

He nodded. "We thought about taking a trip together. We went so far as the planning stage. But it never happened."

"Why not?"

"Because we called it off. Isn't it obvious?"

"And the necklace?"

"As you suspect, I meant to give it to her. Of course, that got called off, too. Along with the rest of it."

"Did you keep anything else of Hatsumi Hidaka's?"

Osamu Nonoguchi thought a moment. "There's a paisley necktie in one of my drawers. That was a present from her. That, and the Meissen teacup in the cupboard. She used it whenever she came to visit. We went to the shop together and picked it out."

"What was the name of that shop?"

"Some place in Ginza, but I don't remember the name or the exact location."

I made sure that Detective Makimura had made a note of

that before asking, "Would it be safe to say that you still haven't forgotten Hatsumi Hidaka even now?"

"I haven't forgotten her, but it was an awful long time ago."

"Then why store those mementos, those memories of her, so carefully?"

"I wouldn't call it 'carefully.' You're overthinking things again. I just never threw them away, and time passed."

"The photos, too? You just forgot to throw out that picture of her you were using as a bookmark in your dictionary?"

Nonoguchi had a difficult time answering that one. Finally he managed, "Imagine what you will. Just . . . it's not related to the murder."

"Not to sound like a broken record, but that's for us to decide."

One more thing I needed to bring up before we left: the accident. I asked him what he thought about it.

"What do you mean what I thought about it? It was sad. And a shock. That's all."

"You must've been angry with Mr. Sekikawa?"

"Sekikawa? Who's that?"

"Tatsuo Sekikawa. I'm sure you've at least heard the name."

"Nope. Never heard it."

I waited for that denial before telling him, "The truck driver. The man who hit Hatsumi."

Nonoguchi looked truly taken aback. "Oh. So that's his name."

"Should we take the fact that you didn't even know his name to mean that you weren't upset with him?"

"No, I just didn't remember his name. Of course I'm upset

with him. Not that me being angry will do anything to bring
her back."

"Is the reason you're not mad at the driver because, at the
time, you thought it was suicide?"

Nonoguchi's eyes went wider. "Why would you think
that?"

"Because you told someone you thought it was."

Apparently I wasn't vague enough, as he seemed to know
immediately to whom I was referring.

"Look . . . it wasn't the most prudent thing to say, but you
shouldn't take it too seriously. It was just something that
popped into my head."

"Even so, I'd like to know why."

"I forget. You try explaining every little thing you've said
over the last five years—I doubt even you would be able to
give clear answers!"

With that, we wrapped up our conversation. I promised
Nonoguchi that we would talk again soon, and we left the hospital room.

Personally, I was elated. I had as good a confirmation as I
could hope for that Osamu Nonoguchi did believe Hatsumi
Hidaka's death was a suicide.

No sooner had we returned to the office than a call came in
from Rie Hidaka. Her things had arrived back from Canada,
and she'd discovered several of Kunihiko Hidaka's videotapes
among them. We left immediately.

"These are all the tapes I found." She'd arranged seven
8 mm videotapes in a line on the table. Each of them repre-

sented an hour of recorded time. I picked up each tape in turn. The cases were numbered one through seven, with no other noticeable titles. Either Hidaka had some system for keeping them straight, or he just remembered their contents.

I asked Rie if she had watched any of the tapes.

She hadn't. "It just didn't feel right."

I asked if we could borrow the tapes for a while and she nodded in agreement.

"There was one other thing I thought you should see. Here." She laid a square paper box about the size of a lunchbox on the table. "It was in with my husband's clothes. I've never seen it before, so he must have been the one who put it in there."

I pulled the box toward me and removed the lid. Inside was a knife wrapped in plastic. It had a sturdy-looking handle, and the blade was at least twenty centimeters long. I picked it up without taking it out of the bag. It was heavy in my hand.

I asked Rie if she knew what the knife had been used for. She shook her head. "I've no idea, that's why I wanted you to see it. Kunihiko never mentioned it to me."

I examined the surface of the knife through the bag. It was not considerably worn, but it definitely wasn't new. I asked if Kunihiko Hidaka ever went mountain climbing, but she replied that, to her knowledge, he hadn't.

I took the knife back with us to Homicide, along with the tapes. We split the videotapes up between us and began watching. The one I got showed some traditional arts in Kyoto, in particular the production of Nishijin textiles: endless footage of craftsmen weaving, their ancient techniques, and snippets of their daily lives. Occasionally a hushed voice would whisper commentary over the image—a voice I assumed to be that of the late Kunihiko Hidaka himself. Roughly 80 percent of my hour-long tape contained footage. The remainder was blank.

When I compared notes with the other detectives, I learned that all the other tapes were pretty much the same thing. Nothing was in them other than research footage for Hidaka's writing. Just to be sure, we traded tapes and looked through each other's on fast-forward, but our impressions remained the same.

I had assumed that Osamu Nonoguchi wanted the video-tapes from Kunihiko Hidaka because something on them was of particular importance, something he didn't want us to see. Yet nothing on the seven tapes seemed to link them to Nono-guchi at all.

A dark mood spread through the office: we had missed our mark. That was when word came from forensics that they had finished examining the knife.

They reported, "Slight wear was found on the blade, showing it had been used at least a couple of times. No traces of anything resembling blood were found. There were several fingerprints found on the handle, which we have identified as belonging to Osamu Nonoguchi."

This was something. Why would Kunihiko Hidaka have a knife bearing Osamu Nonoguchi's fingerprints tucked away like some valuable treasure? And why did he keep this a secret from his wife, Rie? A possible scenario occurred to me at once, but it was so outlandish, I hesitated to voice it without further evidence.

I thought about asking Nonoguchi about the knife, but I rejected that summarily. Without anyone's actually saying it aloud, we all thought this knife would be the trump card we needed to finally break him—we just had to be careful about how we played it.

The next day, we got another call from Rie Hidaka. She'd found another tape. We quickly went over to retrieve it.

"Take a look at this." She held a book out to me—a paperback copy of *Sea Ghost*, the same book she'd given me before.

I gave her a curious look.

"Open the cover."

I lifted the edge of the cover. Detective Makimura gasped. The inside of the book was hollowed out, creating a compartment in which a videotape was concealed. It was like something from an old spy novel.

"This book was packed in a different box from the other books, which I thought was curious. So I took a closer look at it," Rie Hidaka told us.

I asked if she had a video player at the house. When she said yes, I decided to watch it there. Taking it back to the office felt like a waste of time.

The first thing that appeared on the screen was a familiar-looking garden and window. It was the Hidakas' backyard. The video had been taken at night, and it was dark, except for the bright square of the window in the middle.

In the corner of the screen, numbers showed the date and time the video had been taken. It was December, seven years ago.

I leaned forward with anticipation. But the camera only

showed the same garden and window. Nothing happened. No one walked into the frame.

"Shall I fast-forward it a bit?" Detective Makimura asked.

Then a lone figure appeared on-screen.

5

CONFESSION

OSAMU NONOGUCHI'S ACCOUNT

For several days I'd had the feeling that the next time Detective Kaga paid a visit to my hospital bed, he'd bring with him all the answers he'd been looking for. Based on what I'd seen of his work so far, it seemed likely: he was precise, thorough, and startlingly fast. Whenever I closed my eyes, I could hear his footsteps' swift approach. When he found out about Hatsumi, I resigned myself—at least partially—to what was to come. His eyes were far keener than I'd expected. I'm hardly qualified to pass judgment on others, but I think he made the right decision by getting out of teaching.

When next he did come, Kaga was bearing two pieces of evidence. One was a knife, the other, a videotape. To my surprise, the tape was inside a hollowed-out copy of *Sea Ghost*. *How like Hidaka's sense of humor,* I thought. Though one could also interpret it as a tactical move. Had it been any other book, even Detective Kaga might not have arrived at the truth so quickly.

"Please explain what we found on this tape. If you'd like to look at it, I'm sure the hospital has a player we can borrow."

That was all he needed to say to get the full story out of me because nothing less than the truth would explain the scene captured on that tape.

Yes, I still offered some resistance—refusing to answer, even though I knew it was in vain and wouldn't put him off. When he saw me clam up, Detective Kaga wasted no time and began relating his own theory. Clearly he'd expected this to happen, and with the exception of a few details, he nailed it.

By way of an epilogue he added, "All I've said is pure conjecture at this point. However we feel this is enough to construct a viable motive for your crime. You told me that we were free to create our own motive? Well, I think this will do nicely."

It was true. If the only other option was confessing the real reason I killed Kunihiko Hidaka, I'd have been perfectly willing to let them make up something. Of course, I'd never dreamed that the story Detective Kaga would "make up" would be the truth.

"It looks like I've lost," I said after a few moments of stunned silence. I spoke calmly, in an attempt to mask my bewilderment. In this, too, I failed.

"Will you talk?" he asked.

"If I don't, you'll submit what you just told me to the court?"

"Yes."

"Then I'll talk. Since the cat's out of the bag anyway, I'd feel better if all the details were correct."

"Did I get some of it wrong?"

"Hardly anything. It's quite impressive. Still, there are a few details that should be included. It's a matter of honor."

"Your honor?"

I shook my head. "Hatsumi Hidaka's honor."

Detective Kaga nodded. He instructed the detective with him to take notes.

"Hold on a moment," I said. "Do we absolutely have to do it this way?"

"What do you mean?"

"Just . . . it's a long story, and there are parts of it I'd like to get straight in my head. I wouldn't want things to get jumbled in the telling and detract from the story."

"I'll let you look at the finished report."

"I know, but indulge me. If I'm to confess, I'd like to do it in my own words."

Detective Kaga was silent for a moment. Then, finally, he asked, "You mean you'd like to write your own confession?"

"If you'll allow it, yes."

"Very well. That works out better for us anyway. How long will it take?"

"A full day, I should think."

Detective Kaga looked at his watch. "I'll be back tomorrow evening." He stood up and they left the room.

That is how I came to write my own confession. I'm working under the assumption that this will be the last full piece I write. You might call it my final opus. When I think of it in this way, I find myself not wanting to waste a single word; yet unfortunately, I lack the time to labor over every turn of phrase.

My reunion with Kunihiko Hidaka came, as I've said, seven years ago. At the time, Hidaka had already made his authorial debut. He had received a small publisher's new-author award two years prior to our meeting. By the time our paths crossed again, he'd published one collection of short stories and three novels. I believe the publisher lauded him as "a brilliant new voice." Of course, they always say that.

I'd had my eye on him ever since his books started hitting the shelves. Half of me was proud that my childhood friend had made it, while the other half was envious of his success. We'd often talked about becoming writers when we were kids. We both loved books and were constantly recommending our favorites to each other, reading and swapping them when we were finished. Hidaka turned me on to Sherlock Holmes and Arsène Lupin. In return, I gave him Jules Verne.

Hidaka often boasted he would become a better writer than any of them. He was never one for modesty. Though I might never have said it quite as loudly, I shared his dream. So you can see why I was a little jealous of him for having made it out of the gate first, while I hadn't even taken the first step.

I did genuinely want to congratulate him on his success. More selfishly, I also thought connecting with him would offer me a chance. Through Hidaka, I could reach out to publishers, accessing the publishing industry in a way I'd only dreamed of.

I wanted to contact him immediately, but worried that, so soon after his debut, even words of encouragement from an old friend would be nothing more than a nuisance. So, I cheered him on in silence, reading his stories in the magazines and buying his books whenever a new one came out. In the meantime, inspired by his success, I returned to writing in earnest for the first time since a little bit of light fiction I'd written back in college.

I'd been incubating several ideas for years. I chose one

and began to write—a story about a fireworks maker, based on an old man who lived near my house when I was growing up. I visited him several times in the last two years of elementary school and never forgot the fascinating story of how he'd discovered his craft late in life—a salaryman who became enchanted with fireworks after watching a display while on a business trip. It occurred to me that I could expand on that story and make it into a longer work. This became a novel I entitled *A Circle of Fire*.

Two years had passed when I finally decided to write to Hidaka, telling him I'd read everything he'd written and was a strong supporter of his work. I ended by saying I'd like to meet up with him sometime. To my surprise, his response came right away. He called me.

He remembered our childhood days with fondness. Thinking about it now, I realize that was the first time I'd spoken with him at any length since we went off to separate high schools.

"I heard from my mom you'd taken up teaching. Sounds like a nice, steady job. Better than me. I don't get a salary or bonuses. I never know what tomorrow's going to bring." He laughed an easy laugh. Easy because he knew inside he'd gotten the better deal. Still, I didn't hold that against him.

We made plans to meet. We picked the place: a café in Shinjuku; and after that, dinner at a Chinese restaurant. I went to our reunion straight from work, still wearing my suit. He was in jeans and a bomber jacket. I remember thinking, *So that's what it's like to be self-employed,* and for some reason, at the time, it impressed me.

We talked about old times and mutual friends, and

gradually the conversation turned to Hidaka's novels. When he found out that I really *had* read everything he'd written, he was genuinely surprised. According to him, not even the editors who badgered him to write more had read half of his stuff. Now it was my turn to be surprised.

He was in great spirits and talked nonstop, but his face clouded over a little when I asked about sales.

"Sadly, winning the new-author award from a literary magazine isn't a free ticket to success. You need people talking about your books to really move them off the shelves. Of course, a more prestigious award might have a little more pull. It's hard to say."

It must be tough, I thought, *making it as a writer only to realize your struggle is just beginning.* I believe that even then Hidaka was up against a kind of wall in his career. You might call it a slump. I don't think he had a clear path out of it, either. Of course, at the time, I had no inkling of any of this.

Then I confessed to him that I, too, was writing a novel and hoped to make my own debut soon.

"What, you've got a finished novel?" he asked.

"No, embarrassingly, I'm still working on my first. Soon, though. I'll be done soon."

"Well, bring it by when you finish up! I'll read it, and if I like it, maybe I can introduce you to some editors."

"Really? That's really great of you. Puts the ink in my pen, if you know what I mean. I was worried that without any real connections in publishing, I'd have to start sending in submissions blindly and hope for my own new-author award."

"Oh, don't bother with those. They're a pain in the ass. Half of those things are just luck. If what you wrote doesn't suit the tastes of the underlings reading the slush pile, your novel will simply get cut in the early stages and never even see the light of day."

"I've heard the horror stories."

"Yeah, it's brutal. No, going straight to the editors is the only way."

Before we parted that night, I promised I'd let him know when I was done.

With a concrete goal in my sights, my entire attitude toward writing changed overnight. I'd spent more than a year working on the first half of the novel, but it only took me another month to finish it. It ended up being a medium-length work, just under two hundred pages.

I got a hold of Hidaka and told him I'd finished my book. He told me to send it to him, so I made a photocopy and dropped it in the mail. Then all I had to do was wait. I remember going to work that day entirely unable to focus on my lesson plan.

However, no word came from Hidaka. I figured he was busy and didn't bother him right away. But a part of my mind started to worry that the manuscript I'd sent him was so bad he didn't know what to say. Bleaker and bleaker scenarios began to form in my imagination.

A full month after I'd sent him my book, I finally decided to call. His response was disappointing, but not in the way I'd feared: He hadn't read it yet.

"Sorry. I'm working on a really tough assignment right now and just don't have the time."

What could I say to that? He was a professional author. The man needed to eat.

"Well, that's fine. I'm not in any hurry. You do what you need to do," I said, unsure even as I said it why I was encouraging him to delay even further.

"Sorry. As soon as this is done, I promise to get right to it. I looked over the beginning, it's about a fireworks maker, right?"

"Yeah."

"I'm guessing you based it on that old guy who lived next to the shrine?"

I told him he was right.

"It brought back memories! Anyway, I really want to read it, I just haven't had the time."

"How long do you think that assignment's going to take?"

"Probably another month. At any rate, your book's next on the list. I'll call you right away once I've read it."

I thanked him and hung up, my head full of the responsibilities of a full-time writer. I didn't have a shred of doubt in my mind about Hidaka's good intentions.

Another month passed without word. I didn't want to become a nuisance, but I did want to hear what he thought of my writing. Eventually I gave in to the temptation and called again.

"I'm sorry, I still haven't gotten to it." My heart sank. "This job is taking longer than I thought it would. Can you wait? I'm really sorry about this."

"Well, sure." Frankly, though, it was going to be hard for me to wait any longer. Then I had an idea. "If you're too busy, maybe you could suggest another reader? Maybe an editor?"

His tone suddenly turned dark. "Editors are busy people. I can't go sending them something before I know whether it's good or not. Believe me, they're sick of getting every crappy manuscript making the rounds thrown on their desk. If I'm going to bring anybody to them, I have to read it first. Unless you don't want my opinion? Hey, I'm happy to send it back."

What was I supposed to say to that? "That's not what I meant. I just—it seemed like you were pretty busy, and I thought maybe there was someone else."

"Sorry, but nobody I work with has the time to spend reading some amateur's novel. Hey, but don't worry. I will read it, I promise."

"Okay . . . well, it's in your hands." I hung up.

As I feared, another two weeks passed without any word from him. Steeling myself for another disappointment, I dialed his number.

"Hey, I was just about to phone you." Something a little aloof in his tone worried me immediately.

"Did you read it?"

"Yeah, just finished it a couple of days ago."

I resisted the urge to ask him why he hadn't then called me a couple of days earlier and instead asked, "What did you think?"

"Well, about that . . ." The silence on the line lasted more than a few seconds. "It's hard to talk about over the phone," he said finally. "Why don't you come over. We can chat."

This completely threw me. All I wanted to know was if he liked the book or not. I half felt that I was being led on— except, if he was going to the trouble of inviting me over, that must mean he had taken the time to give it an honest reading and had something of substance in the way of feedback. A little nervously, I agreed.

This is how I first came to visit the Hidakas. I had no idea how that visit would change my life.

He'd just bought the house he would live in until his death. Apparently he'd stashed away quite a bit of money during his time as a salaryman, but I also think an inheritance from his father had a lot to do with it. Still, it was lucky for him that he became a bestselling author soon after that, or I suspect that he wouldn't have been able to make his mortgage payments.

I brought a bottle of scotch with me as a present.

Hidaka greeted me at the door in sweats. Standing next to him was Hatsumi.

Thinking back on it, I realize it was love at first sight. The moment I saw her, I felt something akin to inspiration. Almost a kind of déjà vu. It was as though I were meeting someone I'd always been meant to meet. For a moment I just stared at her, unable to speak.

Hidaka didn't seem to notice my momentary disorientation. He told Hatsumi to make coffee and invited me in to his office.

I was expecting him to launch right into what he thought about my book, but he seemed to be avoiding the topic. We discussed current events, and he asked about my teaching work. Even after Hatsumi brought the coffee, he kept the conversation on different topics until, unable to bear it any longer, I blurted out, "What about my story? If it's no good, please tell it to me straight."

His smile faded. "It's not bad. I like the theme."

"You mean it's not bad, but it's not good?"

"Well, yes. That's what I mean. Good books grab the reader, pull you in. Maybe it's a case of having the right ingredients but lacking the right recipe."

"Well, what part in particular doesn't work?"

"The characters just aren't compelling. And I think it's because the story's a little too . . . pat, tidy even."

"Do you mean it feels contrived? The story and the characters lack dimension?"

"Something like that. Don't get me wrong, for an amateur novel I think it's quite good. The writing's fine, and the story elements are all there. It's just the way those elements are put together isn't compelling enough to grab the reader's attention. Or to get published. Technical skill alone doesn't make a salable product, you know."

I was ready for criticism, but this crushed me. If my story had a specific failing, I could try to fix it, but what did "it's fine, but not compelling" mean? It sounded to me like another way of saying I didn't have talent.

"So maybe I should play around with the story line some more? Try to approach it from a different angle?" I asked, trying to keep my spirits up by focusing on the future.

Hidaka shook his head. "I don't see any point in clinging to the same story. If I were you, I'd give yourself a blank slate. Otherwise you might end up making the same mistake again. My recommendation is you write something completely different."

It wasn't what I wanted to hear, but his advice made sense.

I asked whether, if I wrote another story, he would be willing to read it.

"With pleasure," he said.

I started in on my next novel right away. However, my pen seemed reluctant to write. The first time around, I'd completely lost myself in the writing, but this time, I found every little detail bothered me. Sometimes I would spend an entire hour at my desk torturing myself over a single turn of phrase, trying to make it work. Maybe it was because, this time, I had an audience: Hidaka. In a way, that robbed me of my courage. Maybe this was the difference between an amateur and a professional.

Still, I struggled on. In the meantime, I started visiting Hidaka more frequently. You might say our friendship was revived after having lain dormant for so many years. For me, it was fascinating to hear about his life as a working author, and I think Hidaka enjoyed spending time with someone outside his regular circle of editors. He told me once that ever since he'd become an author, he'd felt increasingly isolated from the world around him.

However, I confess I also had an entirely different reason for wanting to visit. I couldn't wait to see Hatsumi again. In many ways, she was my ideal woman. She always had a warm smile for me, and she looked radiant even in her everyday clothes. I'd never seen her all done up, and she might actually have been a knockout. That, after all, would be more Hidaka's style. To me, however, she had a simple charm, something much closer to home: an everyday kind of beauty that other women could only dream of.

On one occasion, I visited without calling ahead. My excuse was that I was in the neighborhood and just dropped by. But in truth, I'd been working at home when I was overcome with a sudden desire to see that smile again. I arrived to find that Hidaka wasn't there. I told myself I was just going to say hello and then go home, since my cover story was that I'd come to see him.

However, to my great surprise, Hatsumi asked me to

come in and visit. She said she'd just finished baking a cake and wanted me to taste it for her. I mumbled something about not imposing on her, but I couldn't pass up the opportunity. I practically fell over myself to accept her invitation.

The following two hours were some of the happiest of my life. I was euphoric and must have talked up a storm. She never frowned at my exuberance, but instead laughed in that bright, girlish way of hers, which sent me even further over the moon. I must have been flushed with excitement because, once I finally left and started to make my way home, I remember how good the cool air felt against my skin.

I continued to drop by, under the pretext of getting writing advice from Hidaka, just to see Hatsumi. Hidaka didn't seem to notice a thing. He had his own reasons for wanting to see me, but I didn't learn of those until a while later.

Finally, I finished my second novel. Again, I wanted Hidaka to read it and give me his opinion. Again, I was disappointed. He didn't like it.

"It just feels like the same old love story," he told me. "Stories about young men falling for older women are a dime a dozen. You need a new twist to make it work. Also, the woman he's supposed to be falling in love with doesn't really work. The character just doesn't feel real. I'm mean, it's obvious you're not writing from personal experience."

I think that's what you'd call a harsh review. I was in shock. The worst part was what he said about the woman. The model for my unreal heroine was none other than Hatsumi herself.

I asked Hidaka if he thought I just didn't have what it took to be a professional writer.

He thought for a moment before saying, "What's the

rush? You have a day job. Keep writing as a hobby. Don't worry about getting your first book published so fast."

His advice did little to console me. I was quite fond of what I'd created with my second novel. Now I was worried about what I might be lacking as a writer. Even Hatsumi's kind words of encouragement were not the salve I needed.

For several days I had difficulty sleeping, and as a result my health quickly deteriorated. I caught a cold and eventually got so sick I couldn't get out of bed. At times like these one really feels the harshness of living alone. I curled up in bed, wrapped in a cold blanket of misery.

Then I had the most unexpected turn of fortune, as I have already told Detective Kaga. Hatsumi came to visit me at my apartment. When I looked through the peephole in my apartment door, I thought for a moment that my fever had peaked and I was hallucinating.

"I heard from my husband that you'd caught a cold and couldn't even go in to work," she told me.

She hardly seemed to notice my excitement at seeing her and went straight into the kitchen, where she began preparing a meal. She'd brought all the ingredients with her. I felt as if I were walking on clouds, and not because of the fever.

The vegetable soup Hatsumi made for me was exceptional. Not that I could taste it at all. It was just that she'd come there for me, that she had cooked it for me. That made me the happiest man alive that night.

I had to take an entire week off work. I was never the healthiest guy, and it often took me a while to recover from colds; but this was the first time I was grateful for my poor constitution. During that week, Hatsumi came over to my apartment three times. On her last visit, I asked her whether it had been Hidaka's idea that she come take care of me.

"Actually, I haven't told him," she said.

"Why not?"

"Well, you know, he's—" She stopped. "Please don't tell my husband. I don't think he'd understand."

"Fine by me." I wanted to know what she was thinking, but decided not to push it.

Once I was back on my feet, I wanted to find a way to thank her. I realized giving her a present might raise eyebrows, so I invited her out to dinner.

She seemed hesitant at first, but eventually agreed. Hidaka was due to be away doing research for some project, and she asked me if that would be a good time. It was better than good; it was perfect.

We had dinner at a traditional Japanese place in Roppongi. That night, she came back with me to my apartment.

I believe I previously described our relationship as a fleeting passion. I'd like to correct that statement now. We loved each other from the bottom of our hearts. For me, there was nothing fleeting or momentary about it. From the first time I laid eyes upon her I felt that she was the woman destiny had meant me to meet. That night was the beginning of our love.

The hours flew by; yet toward the end, Hatsumi told me something shocking about her husband: "He's trying to hold you down, you know." A terrible sadness was in her voice.

"What do you mean?"

"He's trying to keep you from getting published. He wants you to give up writing."

"Because my novels are boring!"

"No, that's not it at all. In fact, I think it's the opposite. He's jealous because the books you write are better than his."

"No way."

"I didn't want to believe it myself. But there's just no other way to explain how he's acting."

"How is he acting?"

"Well, for instance, when you sent him your first novel, I don't think he ever intended to read it seriously—not at first. He suggested that reading some amateur's boring work would throw off his own writing. He said he'd just skim it and tell you whatever you wanted to hear."

"You can't be serious." What she was telling me was so different from what I'd heard from Hidaka himself. "But, he did read it?"

"That's just it. Once he started reading, he couldn't stop. He gives up on things easily, you know. If something strikes him as even a little bit boring, he tosses it away. But there was an . . . *intensity* in the way he read that book. I think it must've been because the world you created grabbed him in a way he couldn't ignore."

"But he said it wasn't professional-level work."

"I don't think he was being honest. I know for a fact he lied to you several times when you called him and he told you he hadn't read it yet. I think he was still deciding what to do. Eventually, he must have decided to disparage your work and discourage you from continuing writing."

"Maybe . . . ," I said, still not believing what I was hearing, "maybe he read it so intently because we were friends."

"No. That's not him. That man isn't interested in any-thing other than himself."

This didn't sound like the sort of thing a wife would say about the husband she'd married after a whirlwind romance. Yet, in retrospect, I wonder if she was looking to me for com-fort because she'd grown disillusioned with the man she'd wed. It's not a thought I care to linger over.

Hatsumi told me that Hidaka had been having trouble with his writing lately and was frustrated at his inability to produce more. Bereft of ideas, his confidence had wavered. That made it even harder to watch an amateur such as myself produce better material.

"I think you should stop bringing your work to my hus-band. Look for someone who will be honest and supportive."

"But wait. If Hidaka really wanted to prevent me from being published, why didn't he just cut me off? Why even read my second book?"

"You don't understand my husband. He isn't giving it to you straight because he wants to prevent you from talking to anyone else. He's trying to make you worry and lose confi-dence in yourself. Not only that, he's stringing you on. He has no intention of ever introducing you to any of his editors." Her voice sounded unusually harsh.

I found it hard to believe Hidaka could be so malicious. Yet I couldn't believe that Hatsumi was making it up. I told her I wouldn't do anything immediately; instead I'd give it some time and see how things developed. She didn't seem satisfied with that, but she didn't press me.

I visited the Hidakas less after that. Not because I no

longer trusted Hidaka, but because I no longer trusted myself to be able to successfully pretend there was nothing between me and his wife. Hidaka had always had a keen eye, and I knew if he caught a meaningful glance, he'd be onto us.

Yet it was hard to go such a long time without seeing her. It was too dangerous for us to meet in public, so after we discussed it in secret, we decided she would come over and visit me at my apartment. As Detective Kaga knows, my apartment building has plenty of empty units, and people probably wouldn't even notice anyone visiting my place. Even if they did, no one knew who Hatsumi was or would recognize her if they did, so there wasn't a big risk that rumors would start to spread.

Hatsumi would wait for Hidaka to be out of town on one of his trips before coming to my place. Though she didn't ever spend the night, she often made dinner for us, which we would eat together. On these occasions, she would wear her favorite apron. (Yes, the apron that Detective Kaga found in my apartment.) When I saw her wearing an apron and standing in my kitchen, I couldn't help but pretend that we were newlyweds, just moved into our new home.

As much as our time together was full of happiness, our partings were miserable. Whenever the time came for her to go back home, we would both become taciturn, shooting reproachful looks at the clock on the wall.

I often thought how wonderful it would be if we could spend two or three days alone together. We even talked about it, although I think both of us knew it was impossible. That is, until an opportunity came along that we couldn't afford to pass up. Hidaka was scheduled to go to America on an assignment for a whole week. He was going with one of his editors, and Hatsumi would be staying at home.

This was what we'd been waiting for. We talked endlessly about how we could spend our time together, giggling like schoolchildren. Eventually, we decided on a trip to Okinawa. I even went to a travel agent and paid for the tickets. It would only be for a short time, but on that trip, we would be husband and wife. I was delirious with joy.

In retrospect, I think our happiness peaked during those days of anticipation. As you know, the trip to Okinawa never happened. The magazine canceled Hidaka's assignment only a few days before he was supposed to leave for America. I don't know the details. Hidaka was crestfallen, but his disappointment was nothing compared to our despair.

To be so close to paradise, only to have it ripped from under my feet, made me mad with desire and determined to see her. As much as this had been true before, now I was even more driven. Our meetings felt too brief, and as soon as we parted, I needed to be with her again.

Yet, her visits dropped off sharply. When I asked why, her answer made me blanch. She was afraid her husband was onto us. Then she said the thing I feared most of all. She thought we should probably end our affair.

"If he finds out about us, he'll take revenge somehow. I can't let you suffer because of me."

"I don't care about that," I told her; but in truth, I didn't want her to suffer, either. Given what I knew of Hidaka's character, I didn't think he'd be eager to sign any divorce papers. Still, I couldn't imagine letting her go.

I struggled with this for several days, letting my teaching duties fall by the wayside as I turned an endless series of plans over in my mind. Finally, I decided. Detective Kaga has already figured out what plan I settled on. I decided to kill Hidaka.

Writing it like that makes it sound like the strangest thing in the world. Yet I was quite sure of myself and hardly wavered at all once I'd made up my mind. In the interest of full disclosure, I should confess that on numerous occasions before then I'd hoped Hidaka would die. I couldn't bear his being married to my Hatsumi. I suppose that only shows how self-delusional we humans can be, since I was clearly the one intruding on someone else's territory. Still, as often as I'd hoped Hidaka would die, until that moment I never imagined killing him with my own hands.

As one might expect, Hatsumi was strongly opposed to my idea. She cried, saying she couldn't let me do something like that. The crime was too great, and the potential punishment too severe. Yet her tears only heightened my madness. I began to feel I truly had no other choice.

"Don't even think about helping," I told her. "I'm doing this by myself. If I fail, if the police take me in, I'll make sure nothing ever implicates you." You might argue that, by this point, I'd lost the capacity for rational thought.

Perhaps because she had realized I was determined, or perhaps because she knew there was no other way for us to be together, Hatsumi eventually agreed. She even insisted on taking part. I didn't want her to endanger herself, but she made her opinion clear: we'd do it together, or not at all.

Together we planned the death of Kunihiko Hidaka. It was not, I feel, a competent plan.

We decided to make it look like the work of a thief. December 13 was to be the day.

I waited until late at night, then snuck into Hidaka's garden. Detective Kaga already knows what I was wearing at the time: black pants and a black jacket. If I had worn a mask, I might not be here now, writing this confession. Yet at the time, it never crossed my mind.

The lights in Hidaka's office were out. Fearfully, I put my hand to the window and pushed the sash to one side. It slid open easily. Holding my breath, I crept inside the room.

I could see Hidaka lying on the sofa in the corner. He was lying on his back, eyes closed, breath regular, sound asleep. We'd picked that night to carry out our plan because he had work due the next day, and Hatsumi knew he was likely to spend the entire night in his office.

I should explain why he was sleeping even though he was on deadline. Hatsumi had mixed sleeping pills in with his dinner. Hidaka used these sleeping pills from time to time, so even if an autopsy found them in his bloodstream, no eyebrows would be raised. When I saw Hidaka lying there, I knew everything was going according to plan. Hidaka had been working when fatigue suddenly crept over him, and he lay down on the sofa, surrendering himself to sleep. Hatsumi came in to check on him, saw him sleeping, and turned off the lights in the office, first making sure that the window was unlocked.

The rest was up to me. With a trembling hand, I pulled the knife from my jacket pocket—the same knife the detectives found among Hidaka's belongings.

To be honest, I preferred strangulation. Just picturing myself stabbing him terrified me. Yet I thought that using a knife would be far more believable. What burglar worth his salt would break into someone's house without a proper weapon?

I wasn't entirely sure where the best place to stab him was. Standing there over him, I decided on the chest. I took off the gloves I'd been wearing, to get a better grip on the knife handle. After all, I reasoned, I could wipe my fingerprints off later. Then, grasping the knife in both hands, I brought it up over my head, ready to plunge it into Hidaka's heart.

That very instant, something unbelievable happened. Hidaka's eyes opened.

I froze. I couldn't swing the knife. I couldn't even speak.

Hidaka, however, moved quickly. By the time I knew what was happening, he was pushing me facedown into the carpet. The knife was already out of my hands. I remember the thought that he'd always been more of an athlete than I was flashing through my mind.

"What's this all about? Why are you trying to kill me?" Hidaka yelled.

But I had no reply.

Eventually he shouted for Hatsumi. I turned my head to see her as she came in, face pale. She must've realized what had happened the instant she heard him call.

"Call the police, there's been an attempted murder!" Hidaka barked.

Hatsumi didn't move.

"What's wrong? Don't stand there fidgeting. Get the phone!"

"But, that's Mr. Nonoguchi."

"I know who it is! But that doesn't change the fact that he tried to kill me!"

"No, Kunihiko. It wasn't him—" Hatsumi began, about to admit her complicity.

Hidaka cut her off. "Do you think I'm stupid?"

I don't know how, but Hidaka had caught on to our whole plan. He'd only been pretending to sleep, waiting for me to do something irrevocable, to make my move, before he leapt into action.

"Hey, Nonoguchi," he said, pressing my face down into the carpet, "you ever read the laws about home invasion? There's a bit in there about the right to self-defense. That means that if you come onto my property with the intent to harm me, and I mistakenly kill you, I don't get in trouble. That seems a lot like the situation we have here now. I could kill you and no one would say a word."

His icy tone sent shivers through my body. Even though I didn't believe he would actually do it, I started to dread what he would do instead.

"However, lucky for you, I'm in a generous mood. And frankly, killing you does nothing for me. Guess I'll just turn you over to the police—" He looked over at Hatsumi and smiled before turning his sharp eyes back to me. "But how would having you in prison do me any good either?"

I had no idea what he was getting at, which made it even more unpleasant.

I felt his grip soften and a moment later he stood up, releasing me. He went over and picked up the fallen knife with a blanket from the sofa wrapped around his hand.

"Rejoice, Nonoguchi. I'm letting you go. You can leave through that window." He was grinning. "You look like you've seen a ghost. Now you'd better leave before I change my mind."

"What are you thinking?" My voice was trembling.

"That's not your concern right now. Leave. Oh"—he brandished the knife—"I'm keeping this as evidence."

I wondered if that knife would hold up as evidence, even with my fingerprints on it. It seemed he'd anticipated my thought, because he added, "You should know this knife isn't my only evidence. I have another trick up my sleeve—something you'll never be able to explain your way out of. I'll even show it to you, when the time is right."

I wondered what he could possibly be talking about, but I didn't dwell on it then. Instead I looked at Hatsumi. Her face was white, with only the edges of her eyes gleaming red. I don't think I'd ever seen a person look so sad before. Nor have I since.

I climbed back out the window and made my way home in a haze. Several times, I thought about running, just disappearing entirely. But I didn't because I was worried about what would happen to Hatsumi.

I spent my days in fear. There wasn't a chance in the world that Hidaka would forgo his revenge. Yet not knowing what form that revenge would take made me all the more terrified. I no longer went to the Hidakas, nor did I see Hatsumi. Our only communication was a furtive phone call she made when he'd stepped out for work.

"He doesn't talk about that night at all," she confided to me. "It's like he's forgotten all about it."

Of course, we both knew he hadn't. I grew even more uneasy.

Several months later I finally learned the nature of his revenge. I discovered it in a bookshop. As I'm sure Detective

Kaga will have realized by now, it was none other than Hidaka's breakthrough novel, *An Unburning Flame*. He had taken the novella I had first shown him and expanded it into his masterpiece.

I couldn't believe it, I didn't want to believe it. It was a nightmare. For me, who had dreamed of becoming an author for so long, it was like having my heart torn to shreds. Only Hidaka could have devised a punishment so cruel and shocking.

To an author, his writing is a part of himself. In many ways, it's his child. As parents love their children, so do authors love the work they create.

But Hidaka had stolen my work from me. Once he published it under his own name, *An Unburning Flame* would forever be known as a novel by Kunihiko Hidaka. Unless I said something, but Hidaka knew I would never do that.

That's right. Even though I'd been badly bruised, I held my tongue. I knew that if I made the slightest sound, he'd say, "Be quiet or you'll go to jail."

If I was going to expose his plagiarism, I'd have to be prepared to admit I'd snuck into his house and tried to kill him.

I thought about turning myself in to the police and, at the same time, announcing that *An Unburning Flame* was mine. I thought about it constantly. Once I even picked up the phone and started to dial the local police station. But in the end, I didn't. A small part of it was that I was afraid of being arrested for attempted murder. But it was mostly because I was terrified that Hatsumi would be charged as my accomplice. I knew that no matter how much I insisted I'd done it all myself, the cops would realize I'd needed help to get as far as I did, and she was the only one who could have done that. Besides, I couldn't

picture Hidaka letting her get away with it. Either way, there
was no way to keep her safe if I confessed. So I let him publish
my work. Even though the pain made a wreck of me, I couldn't
risk any more misfortune coming to Hatsumi on my account.
I'm sure Detective Kaga is laughing to himself as he reads
this. Here I am, a confessed murderer, trying to make myself
look noble. I'm sure that I was more than a little self-delusional
at the time. Yet I needed that delusion to keep me from going
even more insane.

Hatsumi had no words to ease my suffering. She would
occasionally call when Hidaka was out, but the phone calls
were just long stretches of painful silence, interrupted by mean-
ingless, empty words.

"I never imagined he'd do something so horrible. To steal
your work, it's—"

"It's okay. There's nothing either of us can do about it."

"But I feel so bad about it. . . ."

"It's not your fault. I was a fool, that's all. I've reaped what
I sowed."

These chats with the woman I should have loved did
nothing to lift my spirits or give me hope. I just felt my heart
sinking lower and lower.

As fate would have it, *An Unburning Flame* was well received. Every time I saw it featured in a magazine or a newspaper, I felt as if something were chewing away at my heart. For
a fleeting moment, I was happy to see the work praised. But
then I'd snap back to reality and realize that as far as anyone
else knew, it wasn't my work being praised.

On the strength of this book, Hidaka went from being
talked about everywhere to receiving a prestigious literary

award. I wonder if anyone can understand my pain when I saw his face beaming proudly from the pages of the newspapers. I wasn't able to sleep for several nights.

My nightmare continued unabated until one day my doorbell rang. When I looked through the peephole, I thought I might choke. Standing on the other side of my door was Kunihiko Hidaka. It was the first time I'd seen him in person since the night I broke into his house. Even though I hated him for stealing my work, the guilt I felt for what I'd done was stronger. For a second, I wondered if I should pretend not to be at home.

Finally I realized there was nothing to gain by running away, so I opened the door.

Hidaka smiled thinly. "Were you sleeping?"

"No." It was Sunday. I was still in my pajamas.

"Great, I wouldn't want to interrupt your beauty sleep." He took a look inside. "Mind if I come in? There's something I want to talk to you about."

"Sure . . . I haven't cleaned up in a while."

"I don't mind. It's not like we're taking publicity photos."

Not like the publicity photos all the newspapers were taking of him.

"Also"—he looked at me—"I thought you might have something on your mind. Something you wanted to talk to me about."

I said nothing.

We sat facing each other on the living-room sofa. Hidaka took a long look around my apartment. I grew nervous, afraid that he might spot something of Hatsumi's. I was glad I'd washed her apron and put it away.

"The place looks pretty tidy for a bachelor pad," he said finally.

"I guess."

"Do you have someone come in and clean up for you?"

I looked at him, startled. He still had that same cold smile on his face. It was clear what he was suggesting.

"What did you want to talk about?"

"Don't be in such a rush." He lit a cigarette. He began making small talk, something about the latest political scandal. I'm sure he was doing it just to see me sweat.

I was on the verge of raising my voice when he said, in the same casual tone, "So, about *An Unburning Flame* . . ."

I straightened up on the sofa, waiting for his next words.

"I thought I should apologize for the similarities to that piece you wrote, coincidental though they are. What was your book called again? *A Circle of Fire,* was it?"

I glared at him. I couldn't believe what I'd just heard. Had he no shame? Coincidental similarities? If that wasn't plagiarism, they should remove the word *plagiarism* from the dictionary.

He continued, "And let's be honest. I'm sure there are some parts you can't write off as coincidence. I can't deny that I happened to read your book in the middle of writing my own, and it could well have influenced me. No doubt some things were planted in my subconscious and ended up coming out in the finished work. The same thing happens to composers all the time, you know. Even though they don't mean to, they end up writing a song that sounds a lot like another one."

I listened to him in shocked silence. Did he expect me to believe a word he was saying?

"So that's why I'm glad you didn't raise a fuss when you found out about the book. And you know what, it's good you didn't. We're not strangers and we have a relationship that was built over years. The fact that you didn't do anything impulsive, that you remained mature about the whole thing, was really for the best. For both of us."

Translation: You were smart not to raise a fuss. Keep quiet, and in exchange, I won't tell anyone you tried to kill me.

"That's all good, but I really came to talk to you about something else."

I looked up at him, wondering what new insanity he was preparing to unveil.

"A lot of things came together to make *An Unburning Flame* the success that it is. Now a lot of people have read it and more will read it in the future. Not to mention the prize it was awarded. I just thought it would be unfortunate if the momentum was to die out after just one novel."

I could feel the blood drain from my face. He was going to do it again. He was going to use my second book as the basis for his own next novel. He already had a copy at his house.

"So you're going to plagiarize that one, too?"

Hidaka frowned. "Now that's a word I didn't expect to hear from you."

"Why pretend? No one else is here to hear us. You can call it what you want, pretend what you will, but plagiarism is plagiarism."

His face completely calm, Hidaka said, "It appears you don't understand what *plagiarism* means. Look it up in your dictionary. I'm sure you'll find that it says something like 'the use of all or a portion of another person's work, presenting it as your own, without their permission.' You see what I'm getting at? If you use it without permission, it's plagiarism. If you have permission, it's not."

I never gave you permission, I thought. "You're saying that if you use another of my works, you don't want me complaining?"

He shrugged. "You're still misunderstanding me. I'm offering you a deal. A pretty good deal, I might add."

"I know the deal. If I close my eyes to your theft, you won't turn me over to the police and tell them about that night."

"Don't get so hot under the collar. I chose to let you off the hook 'that night.' The deal I'm talking about is more forward thinking."

I didn't see how "forward thinking" or thinking in any direction could possibly save me, but I waited for him to continue, silently watching his lips.

"Look, Nonoguchi, you do have talent. But having talent and actually becoming a published author are two different things. Don't even talk to me about becoming a bestselling author, because that certainly has nothing to do with talent. To get there, you need a special kind of luck. What that luck is, and how to get it, is a hard thing to pin down. Everyone wants it, everybody has a plan to get them there, but it still never goes how you think it will."

I saw the sincerity in his face as he talked, and it occurred to me that he was thinking about his own time as a struggling author.

"I bet you think *An Unburning Flame* made such a big hit because it was a good book, right? I won't deny that it is. But that's not everything. Let me give you an extreme example. What if that book had come out not in my name, but under yours? What if it said Osamu Nonoguchi on the cover instead of Kunihiko Hidaka? Do you think it would have sold?"

"We won't know until we try."

"No, we do know. It wouldn't have gone anywhere. It would've been ignored and soon forgotten. You would've felt like you'd just thrown a pebble into the ocean."

It was a harsh assessment, but I couldn't refute it. I knew too much about the publishing world to do that.

"So you're saying that's why you published it under your own name?" I demanded. "Are you trying to justify doing what you did?"

"What I'm saying is as far as that book is concerned, it was better that it was published under my name. If it hadn't been, not nearly as many people would've read it."

"You act as though you've done me a favor."

"I'm not trying to act like anything. I'm merely telling it like it is. Believe me, there are a disheartening number of conditions that have to be met before a novel can really become a bestseller."

"You think I don't know that?"

"No, you clearly don't. Because if you did, then you'd understand what I'm trying to tell you. See, I want you to become the author Kunihiko Hidaka."

"I'm sorry, I think I misheard you. Did you just say you want me to be you?"

"Don't look so shocked. It's no big deal. Of course, I'll still be me, too. Think of it this way: Kunihiko Hidaka isn't a person's name, it's a trademark we'll use to sell books."

Finally, I understood. "You want me to be your ghost-writer."

"Not my favorite word. It has a ring of cowardice to it. However, you could put it that way, yes."

I glared at him. "You have some nerve, you know that?"

"It's really not that outlandish a request. Like I said, it's not a bad deal for you."

"I can't think of a worse deal."

"Oh? Let's pretend you've written a novel for me to publish. How about, when that novel goes into paperback, I give you twenty-five percent of all royalties. Is it sounding good yet?"

"Twenty-five percent? I'm writing the damn thing and I don't even get half? What kind of terms are those?"

"Well, let me ask you this then. Say you published a book under your own name. How well do you think it would sell? Do you think it would sell more than a quarter of the copies it would sell if it was published under *my* name? Under the name of Kunihiko Hidaka?"

He had a point. I wasn't confident a book published under my own name would sell even a quarter of the copies. It might not even sell a fifth or sixth.

"At any rate," I said, after thinking about this for a while, "I've no intention of selling my soul for cash."

"So you refuse?"

"You're damn right I refuse."

"Well!" Hidaka looked surprised. "I really wasn't expecting that response."

Something about the languid way he said it sent a shiver down my spine. A dark light crept into his eyes.

"I was hoping to keep our relationship civil, but seeing as

how you've no such intentions, I can't go on bending over backward to make things work." Hidaka reached into the bag at his side and pulled out a small, square package. He placed it on the table. "I'll leave this here. I encourage you to watch it once I leave. I'll call soon, and I hope by then you'll have changed your mind."

"What is it?"

"You'll see." Hidaka stood. He left my apartment without saying another word or sparing even a single glance back at me.

After he had left, I sat unmoving on the couch, staring at the package sitting on the table. Finally I picked it up and opened it. It contained a VHS tape. An uneasy feeling crept into my chest as I put the tape in my VCR.

Detective Kaga is already aware of the contents of that tape, but I was seeing it for the first time. I found myself watching a video of the Hidakas' garden. I noticed the date stamp at the bottom right of the screen, and my heart froze. It was the day I'd tried to kill Hidaka.

Eventually, a man appeared on-screen. He was wearing black clothes, so as to better blend into the darkness, but his face was clearly visible. What a farce! Why hadn't I thought to wear a mask?

Anyone could see clearly that the intruder caught on tape was none other than Osamu Nonoguchi. Completely oblivious to the camera, the Nonoguchi on the tape went over to the office window facing the garden and climbed in.

That was the only thing on the tape, but it was enough. Even if I denied the attempted murder, I had no explanation for why I'd tried to sneak into his house.

I sat there numbly, the words Hidaka had said on the night I'd tried to kill him playing through my head. So this tape was his "other piece of evidence."

As I sat there, unsure what to do, the phone rang. It was Hidaka. His timing was perfect, as though he had been watching my every move.

"Did you watch the tape?" I could tell he was enjoying this.

I told him I had.

"So, what did you think?"

"You knew, didn't you?" I said, blurting out the first thing that was on my mind.

"Knew what?"

"You knew I was going to sneak into your office that night. That's why you set up the video camera."

I thought I heard him guffaw. "How the hell would I know that?"

"Well, I—"

"Wait!" he said, cutting me off. "Did you tell someone about your plan? Did someone else know you were coming to kill me that night? If you had, I suppose word could have reached me. They say the walls have ears, you know."

It occurred to me that Hidaka was trying to get me to admit to Hatsumi's complicity. Or rather, since he knew I would never give her up, he was toying with me. I didn't respond.

After a while, he said, "The reason I had that camera running is that I was having trouble with animals getting into my garden and wreaking havoc. I wanted to catch whatever animal was responsible, but I never expected that animal to be you, Nonoguchi."

That story was unbelievable, but I wasn't about to start

an argument over it. "So? What did you hope showing me the video would prove? What do you want me to do?"

"Isn't it obvious? Surely you're not that dense. Oh, I should mention that the tape you have is only a copy. I have the original here safe with me."

"Are you honestly trying to blackmail me into being your ghostwriter? Writing is hard enough when I'm inspired. I can't imagine having to force it." As soon as I said that, I wished I hadn't, because it sounded as if I'd taken the first step toward acquiescing to his demand. Yet what choice did I have?

"Actually, I have faith you'll come around." I could tell from his voice that he thought he'd already won. My defenses were shattered. "I'll call again soon," he said, and hung up.

For the next several weeks I drifted around like a ghost. A ghost *writer*. I had no idea what I was going to do. I went through the motions of going to work, yet teaching was the furthest thing from my mind. Some of the students must've complained because the headmaster called me into his office and chewed me out.

Then, one day in a bookshop, I found it: a blurb in a literary magazine about the new novel from Kunihiko Hidaka, his first since *An Unburning Flame*.

Unable to stop my hands from shaking, I found the book on display and quickly skimmed it. I felt dizzy; I almost collapsed right there in the bookshop. It was as I'd feared. The novel was heavily based on the second book I'd given Hidaka to read.

My whole world was spiraling out of control. I spent weeks chastising myself for my stupidity on the night of the attempted murder. Again, I thought about running away somewhere and disappearing. Yet I lacked the spine. If I wanted to escape Hidaka altogether, I'd have to go far away and not register my new address. That would mean I wouldn't be able to work as a teacher. How would I live? I wasn't in good enough health for physical labor. Never had I felt my own lack of value to society more acutely than I did then. In any case, I couldn't bring myself to leave Hatsumi behind. I imagined her suffering in that house, by his side, and it agonized me.

Hidaka's new novel quickly hit the shelves in paperback and seemed to be selling well. Every time I saw it on the bestseller lists, I felt divided, because somewhere in that ocean of regret inside of me bobbed a tiny acorn of pride. Indeed, when I looked at the situation as objectively as possible, a cold, analytical part of me had to admit that, had I published the book under my own name, it probably wouldn't have sold.

Several more weeks passed until, one Sunday, Hidaka returned. He walked into my apartment as though nothing were the matter and sat down on my sofa.

"As promised," he announced, placing an envelope on the table. I picked it up and looked at it, finding it was stuffed with bills. "That's two million yen. That's almost a year's salary for some people."

"What's this for?"

"I told you, if the book sold, I'd give you your cut. That's a quarter of the royalties, as promised."

I looked inside the envelope again and shook my head. "I told you I wasn't going to sell my soul."

"Don't be so dramatic. Just think of what we're doing as a collaboration. It's not uncommon to collaborate on a novel these days, and you have a right to be paid for your work."

"This isn't collaboration." I stared at Hidaka. "This is rape. You're having your way with me, and then you're trying to pay me off like I was a prostitute."

"How vulgar. And untrue."

"Is it?"

"No one being raped sits still. But you did."

To my shame, I couldn't think of a retort. "Regardless," I said with great effort, "I can't accept this money." I pushed the envelope back toward him.

He looked down at it, but made no move to pick it up. It remained sitting on the table.

"Actually, what I really wanted to talk about was what comes next."

"Tell me then, what does come next?" I said with as much sarcastic faux enthusiasm as I could muster.

"Our next novel. I'm supposed to be writing a serialized story for a monthly magazine. I was hoping we could toss around some ideas."

He said it as though I'd agreed to his terms and to be his ghostwriter.

I shook my head. "You're a writer. You should understand. How am I supposed to think up any kind of story in my current mental state—let alone a good one! You can't force it. It's physically and mentally impossible."

But he didn't back down. Instead, he said something unexpected. "Of course I don't expect you to sit down right now and write something. But surely you could go find something you've already written? That wouldn't be so hard."

"I don't have anything else written. You've already seen everything."

"Don't be coy with me. What about that stuff you wrote for the school magazine?"

"What, that?" I said, truly surprised. "I don't have any of those anymore."

"Bull."

"It's the truth. I got rid of them a long time ago."

"See, I don't believe you. Writers always hang on to their drafts and stories. If you insist, I'd be happy to search your house for them. I'm sure it won't take long. You've probably got them all stashed on a bookshelf or in a desk drawer." He stood and went into the next room.

I panicked. All of my early stories were in spiral-bound notebooks on my bookshelf.

"Wait a second," I called out. "It won't do you any good. I wrote those stories when I was a student. The writing's a mess, the plot structure is all over the place. They're certainly not the work of an adult writer."

"Let me decide that for myself. Besides, I'm not looking for finished works. Just some raw material that I can polish into a salable product. After all, *An Unburning Flame* wouldn't have been one for the literary history books if I hadn't given it my touch."

I couldn't understand how he could be so proud about stealing my work.

I told him to wait on the sofa and went into the next room. Eight of my old notebooks were on the top shelf in my office. I chose one. At that very moment, Hidaka entered the room behind me.

"I told you to wait."

Without a word, he stepped up, snatched the notebook

out of my hand, and quickly leafed through the pages. Then he glanced over at the bookshelf and quickly grabbed the remaining notebooks.

"Trying to trick me, were you?" He grinned. "You picked the notebook with your rough draft of *A Circle of Fire,* didn't you? Did you think you could brush me off with that?"

I bit my lip and looked down at the floor.

"Whatever. I'll be taking these. All of them."

"Hidaka." I looked back up at him. "Aren't you ashamed of yourself? Has the well of your talent run so dry that you feel compelled to steal something I wrote as a student?"

I wanted my words to hurt, even if only a little. It was the best attack I could muster.

And my words did have an effect. Hidaka's eyes flashed and he grabbed me by the collar. "You have no idea what it's like to be an author!"

"You're right, I don't. But I can say this. If it means having to do what you're doing, I don't want to be an author."

"What happened to the dream?"

"I woke up."

He let me go. "You're probably better off for it," he muttered under his breath, and left the room.

"Wait, you forgot something." I picked up the envelope with the 2 million yen in it and held it out to him.

His gaze shifted between my face and the envelope for a moment; then he shrugged and took it.

His serialized novel began two or three months later. I read it, realizing it was based on one of my stories. However, by that time I suppose I'd given up—or at least, I was ready for it, because it didn't come as the same sort of shock the first two books had. I'd already given up ever becoming an author in my own right, so the thought that at least my stories were out there and being read made me glad.

I still received the occasional call from Hatsumi. In our conversations, she would disparage her husband and apologize to me. Once, she said, "If you ever decide to turn yourself in for what happened, I will gladly share whatever punishment comes."

I realized she was telling me this because she knew Hidaka was holding our relationship over my head and she wanted to give me a way out. I almost wept with happiness. Even if we hadn't seen each other for a long time, I felt as though our hearts were still connected.

"You don't have to worry about that," I told her. "I'll do something. I'll find a way out of this."

"But you've already gone through so much." I could hear her crying on the other end of the line.

I tried consoling her, but the truth is, I didn't know what I was going to do. My promise to find a way rang hollow even to my ears, and it made me miserable.

Whenever I think back on that time, I'm filled with regret. I wonder why I didn't do what she suggested. If we'd turned ourselves in, my life would be entirely different now. At the very least, I would not have lost the thing most important to me in this world.

I learned of the accident in the newspaper. Because she was the wife of a bestselling author, the article was more prominent than a typical accident report.

I don't know how deeply the police investigated, but I never heard anyone suggest that Hatsumi's death was anything other than an accident. Yet, from the first moment, I knew that it wasn't. She took her own life. I need hardly say why.

In a sense, I killed her. If I hadn't gone mad and tried to kill Hidaka, none of this would have come to pass.

Call it nihilism, but at the time I was barely alive. I was just going through the motions, an empty shell. I didn't even have the strength to follow Hatsumi into death. I fell ill and was frequently absent from work. Hidaka, however, kept writing. In addition to the novels he wrote using my work as a basis, he also turned out a few originals. I never bothered to find out which of the novels received more praise.

Roughly half a year after Hatsumi's death, I received a package in the mail. The large envelope contained about thirty printed pages. I thought it might be a story, yet when I started reading it, I realized it was something far more sinister. It appeared to be a journal written by Hatsumi, woven together with an account by Hidaka. The journal section described Hatsumi's falling into a special relationship with a man she called N (myself), with whom she eventually conspired to kill her husband. Hidaka's account described in unemotional terms the sorrow of a husband who comes to realize his wife has stopped loving him. Then came the attempted murder. Up to that point, I believe everything was more or less the truth, but what followed was clearly fiction, merely invention. Hatsumi was portrayed as deeply regretting her mistake and begging for forgiveness. Hidaka, in turn, spends long hours talking with her, and together they decide to try again. Just when things are looking up for the couple, Hatsumi has an unfortunate accident. The story ended with her funeral. As a piece of fiction, it wasn't bad. For some readers, it might even have been moving.

I was speechless, and confused. What was I supposed to make of this?

That night, Hidaka called. "You read it?"

"What's this all about? Why did you write this?"

"I was thinking of giving it to my editor next week. It'll probably appear in the magazine next month."

"Are you crazy? Do you know what this would do?"

"I have a pretty good idea," he said, utterly calm.

"If you write that, I'm telling the truth."

"What truth is that?"

"You know as well as I do. That you stole my work."

"Did I now?" he said, entirely unfazed. "And who would believe that? You don't have any proof, do you?"

"Proof?" I gasped. How would I prove he had stolen my work when he had my notebooks? I had copies of my two novels—the ones he'd plagiarized—on my word processor, but what would that prove? That was when I realized that the death of Hatsumi meant the death of the only witness to all that had happened between Hidaka and me.

"Of course, if now doesn't work for you, I don't have to give that story to my editor tomorrow. I could always wait for a better time." I got what he was aiming at before he actually said it. "Fifty pages. Give me a story fifty pages long, and I'll turn that over to my editor instead."

This, then, was his plan. To create a situation in which I'd be forced to write for him. And I had no way to resist. I couldn't let him publish those journal entries. For the sake of Hatsumi's memory, I couldn't.

"When do you need it by?" I asked, my voice flat.

"Next weekend."

"This is the last time?" It was only half a question at best, and he didn't even bother to respond.

"Let me know when you're done." He hung up.

That was the day that I became Kunihiko Hidaka's ghost-writer. Since then, I've written seventeen short stories and three novels for him. These were the computer files the police found.

I'm sure if he's reading this, Detective Kaga must be wondering why I didn't put up more of a fight. To be honest, I'd grown weary of the constant psychological warfare between Hidaka and me. It seemed easier to just write what he needed and, by doing so, keep my past with Hatsumi private.

Oddly enough, over the next two or three years, the relationship between Hidaka and me developed into that of genuine collaborators. He introduced me to a publisher of children's literature because he had no interest in the genre. He also probably felt a little guilty by then. Finally, one day, he said the words I'd been waiting to hear.

"Once this next novel's done, you're free to go. Our working relationship is over."

I couldn't believe my ears. "Really?"

"Really. But I only want you writing books for kids. Stay out of my territory. Understood?"

I thought I was dreaming. One last book and I would be free.

A short while later, I understood the reason behind Hidaka's change of heart. His marriage to Rie was in the works and they were considering moving to Vancouver. In packing up his things, Hidaka clearly wanted to jettison some of his other baggage as well.

I believe I was looking forward to the day the newlyweds moved to Vancouver even more than they were.

Then the day arrived. Bringing a disk with the next installment of *The Gates of Ice* on it, I headed to Hidaka's house. This would be the last time I handed him a computer file. Since I didn't have a computer, after he moved to Canada I would have to send the rest of the manuscript by fax. Once *The Gates of Ice* was done, so were we.

Hidaka was in high spirits when I handed him the disk. I let him rattle on about his new place in Vancouver before asking, "You'll be giving me my things back today, right?"

"What things?" Even though there was no way he'd forgotten, it wasn't in Hidaka's nature to make anything easy.

"My notebooks. You know the ones."

"Notebooks?" He made a show of not understanding, then said, "Ah, I remember. Sorry. It's been a while since I looked at them."

He opened up the drawer to his desk and pulled out eight spiral-bound notebooks.

I clutched the prodigal notebooks to my chest. This, I thought, made us even. Now I would be able to prove his plagiarism.

"You look happy," he said.

"I guess I am."

"Great. Though I wonder—why do you want those notebooks back so badly?"

"Isn't it obvious? These prove that those books you wrote were based on my stories."

"See, that's the thing." He smiled again. "Couldn't someone interpret it the other way around? What if you read the books I published, and then wrote your versions in those note-books based on them?"

"What?" A shiver ran down my spine. "Is that how you'd try to spin it?"

Hidaka looked surprised. "Why would I have to explain myself to anyone? I suppose, if you were to show those to a third party, I might have to say a few words in my own de-fense. It would be up to that third party to decide whom to believe. Not that I want to argue with you about this now, but I want you to understand that having those notebooks doesn't give you an advantage over me—not in the slightest."

"Hidaka"—I glared at him—"I'm not your ghostwriter anymore—"

"I know, I know. *The Gates of Ice* is the last one. That's fine."

"So what's this all about then?"

"Nothing. Just remember: there hasn't been any change in where things stand between us."

When I saw the cold smile on his face, I understood. He had no intention of ever letting me go. When the time came that he needed me, he would use me again.

"Where's the tape and the knife?" I asked.

"What tape and knife?"

"Don't play the fool. You know what I'm talking about."

"Oh those. I have them in a safe place. Only I know where."

At that moment, a knock came at the door. Rie poked her head in and told us that Miyako Fujio was there.

I think Hidaka agreed to see her because he wanted an excuse to shoo me out of his office.

Concealing my anger, I said good-bye to Rie and left the

house. She saw me only as far as the door, as Detective Kaga
so astutely figured out.

Once outside, I went around to the garden and over to
Hidaka's office window. Then I hid beneath the window and
listened while he spoke to Miyako Fujio. As I expected, he was
vague and noncommittal in response to her complaints. Of
course, considering that the novel she had a problem with,
Forbidden Hunting Grounds, was one I'd written, there wasn't
much of substance he could say about it.

Eventually, Fujio departed, obviously irritated. Rie left for
the hotel immediately afterward, and Hidaka stepped out of
his office, apparently to go to the bathroom.

Thinking that this was my chance, I made up my mind to
go after him—to end it once and for all. If I didn't act immediately, I might never be free from Hidaka's clutches.

It was my good fortune that the window was unlocked.
Sneaking in, I waited behind the open door, the brass paperweight clutched in my fist.

I don't need to describe what happened next in detail. Suf-
fice it to say, as soon as he walked in, I hit him in the back of
the head as hard as I could. He crumpled to the floor. I then
strangled him with the phone cord, just to be sure.

What happened from there was just as Detective Kaga
surmised. I created an alibi using Hidaka's computer. The
trick I used was one I'd thought up while plotting out a young-
adult mystery novel. Yes, that's right—it was a trick intended
to fool children. Go ahead and laugh if you like.

Still, I prayed that it would be good enough to elimi-
nate me as a suspect. I prayed that my earlier attempt to murder
Hidaka wouldn't come to light. That's why I asked Rie to let

me know when Hidaka's videotapes were returned from Canada.

Yet Detective Kaga was efficient in uncovering all of my secrets. His keen powers of deduction are impressive, as much as I might loathe them. Not that the detective is in any way to blame.

As I wrote at the beginning of this confession, I was startled to find that the tape bearing the evidence of my folly had been kept in a hollowed-out copy of *Sea Ghost*. *Sea Ghost* is one of the few novels Hidaka wrote himself, and as I'm sure the reader of this account is aware, the scene within the novel describing an attempt on the main character's life by his wife and her lover was based on actual events. I believe that the image of me coming in through the window was the clue that guided Detective Kaga to the truth. Even in death, Hidaka persevered in his efforts to destroy me, and finally he's succeeded.

Now I've said all there is to say. I'm afraid I concealed my motive because I wanted to hide the truth about Hatsumi. I'm sorry for the trouble I've caused, but I hope this account helps you understand how I felt.

I am prepared to accept whatever punishment I am due.

6
THE PAST (PART ONE)
KYOICHIRO KAGA'S NOTES

May 14

Today, I visited the middle school where Nonoguchi taught until recently. Classes had just let out, and the front gates were thronged with students on their way home. Out on the sports field, a few kids were raking the track.

I checked in at the front office and asked if I could speak with any instructors who'd been close to Mr. Nonoguchi. The woman in the office went to talk to another teacher before both of them went back to the teacher's office. The wait was annoying, but I remembered that this was the way things typically worked at public schools. After a wait of almost twenty minutes, they finally brought me to a meeting room.

I met with the school headmaster, a man named Eto, and another man, Fujiwara, who taught composition. I assumed that the headmaster was there to make sure that Fujiwara toed the school-board party line.

I first asked the two men whether they'd heard about Kunihiko Hidaka's murder. They had and, in fact, knew quite a bit of detail. They told me that they knew Nonoguchi had been Hidaka's ghostwriter and had heard that his resentment over this was Nonoguchi's motive for killing him. I got the distinct impression they were eager to hear even more gritty details from me.

I asked if they'd ever noticed anything out of the ordinary during the time that Nonoguchi had been working as a ghostwriter.

After a moment's hesitation, Fujiwara said, "I knew he was writing novels. I'd even read some of his stuff in a children's magazine. But, no, I had no idea he was a ghostwriter. Especially not for a famous author like Hidaka."

"Did you ever witness Mr. Nonoguchi writing anything?"

"No. He kept to his teaching duties while he was at school, so I think he was writing at home, after work, or on the weekends."

"Would you say his teaching load was light enough for him to be able to do that?"

"Well, I wouldn't say that his load at school was particularly light. But he was very clever at getting out of any extracurricular activities at school, and he did go home early every day. Particularly beginning in the fall of last year. It was, well, that he was in poor health, though we never found out exactly what the problem was. I think everyone let him coast on that a bit. Evidently, he was using that extra time to write Kunihiko Hidaka's novels! Pretty impressive, isn't it?"

"You mentioned that he started going home particularly early starting in the fall of last year. Do you have any physical record of this?"

"We don't use time cards or anything here, so no. But I'm pretty sure that's when it started. The composition teachers have a meeting to touch base every two weeks. Around that time he stopped showing up to those."

"But he participated normally until that time?"

"Well, he wasn't the most active of participants, but he was there."

Regarding Osamu Nonoguchi's character:

"He kept to himself, so you'd never really know what he was thinking. I caught him staring out the window more than once. Of course, he must've been really struggling. I don't think he was a bad person, deep down. I think I can understand how, after taking it for years, he just snapped. Not that I'm condoning murder, mind you." Fujiwara smiled. "I've always enjoyed Hidaka's novels—I read quite a few of them. But knowing that it was really Mr. Nonoguchi who wrote them changes how I think of them."

I thanked both of the men and left the school. On my way home, I passed by a large stationery shop. I went inside, showed the woman at the register a photograph of Osamu Nonoguchi, and asked whether he'd come in at all over the last year. She said she thought he looked familiar, but she couldn't remember.

May 15

Today, I went to interview Rie Hidaka. For the past week, she's been staying in an apartment in Yokohama. Presumably she moved to get away from what's been happening. She sounded miserable over the phone, and I suspect that, if I'd been a journalist, she would've refused to see me.

We arranged to meet in a café in a shopping center near her apartment. She told me she didn't want to meet me at her apartment or for me to even come by the building. She was afraid somebody would notice.

The café was right next to a boutique holding an annual bargain sale, but it was set off from the main shopping center thoroughfare in such a way that patrons couldn't be seen from the outside. Inside, the café was cluttered with displays and dividers. All of this made it a good place to talk without being seen or overheard. We sat across from each other at a table in the far back.

I first asked her how she was doing.

She gave me a wry smile. "I've been better. Honestly, I can't wait for this circus to end."

"Whenever there's an investigation it takes a while for things to quiet down."

She shook her head and said, irritated, "I wonder if anyone out there understands that we're the victims here? They're treating this like some kind of celebrity scandal, and the way they talk about it, it's as though my husband was the bad guy."

It was true. The entertainment news shows on television and the weekly magazines were talking more about Kunihiko Hidaka's plagiarism than his murder. With his former wife's adultery added into the mix, tabloids that didn't normally bother with novelists had jumped all over the story.

"You have to just ignore it," I said.

"I've been trying, believe me. If I didn't, I'd lose my mind. Unfortunately, it's not just the media that's the problem."

"Has something happened?"

"Not something, many things. There are the phone calls, and all the letters. Hostile, threatening ones from random people. I don't know how they found their address and phone number, but they're now calling and sending them to my parents' house. I suppose they learned from the news that I'm not staying at our old house anymore."

"Have you reported all this to the police?"

"I have. We all have. But it's not something the police can do much about, is it?"

She was right, though I wasn't inclined to admit it. "What are they saying—the letters, I mean?"

"Oh, lots of things. Some people want me to return all of the royalties his books have earned, and others are just mad, feeling that my husband betrayed them. We've had people send boxes filled with his novels. And there are a lot of letters demanding that we return all the awards he won."

In my opinion, the majority of these people weren't actually fans of her late husband's or even lovers of literature. Many of them, I felt sure, hadn't even heard the name Kunihiko Hidaka before news of his murder broke. I bet the people harassing her got their kicks off others' unhappiness and always had their eyes out for an opportunity to make someone else miserable. It didn't matter who Rie Hidaka was, let alone that she was the victim.

I told Rie this and she agreed.

"Ironically enough, my husband's books still seem to be selling very well. I guess it's mostly morbid curiosity at this point."

I'd heard that Hidaka's book sales were up. However, the only copies of his books on the market were the ones already on bookstore shelves. His various publishers had all issued statements that they wouldn't reprint his books. I assumed the editor who had once refuted the ghostwriter theory had wisely decided to remain publicly silent on the matter.

Then Rie related a bit of surprising news, though she said it casually. "I also got a legal letter from Mr. Nonoguchi's relatives."

"What did it say?"

"They were demanding the profits from my husband's books. They felt they had a right to at least the advances paid for any book based on Mr. Nonoguchi's work. Their representative was Nonoguchi's uncle."

Mr. Nonoguchi was an only child, and both his parents had already died. His uncle was probably the closest living relative. Still, it was an astonishing request to make of the widow on behalf of the man who killed her husband. *It really does take all kinds,* I thought. "How did you reply?"

"I told them my lawyer would contact them."

"Good move."

"Honestly, I'm amazed by all of this. I've never heard of anyone demanding money from the estate of a murder victim!"

"It's an unusual case, and I'm not clear on the legal intricacies myself. Though I'd be very surprised if you had to pay anything."

"As would I. But the money isn't the problem. I can't stand it that everyone seems to think it was my husband's own fault he was killed. And Mr. Nonoguchi's uncle didn't seem one bit sorry."

Rie Hidaka bit her lip and her eyes flared. I was relieved to see she was more angry than sad. I didn't want her breaking into tears in the café.

"I know I told you this before, Detective Kaga, but I still don't believe my husband stole someone else's work. When he would talk about a new book he was writing, his eyes would get so bright—like a child's. I know he truly enjoyed creating stories."

I nodded, understanding how she felt. However, I thought it would be inappropriate for me to tell her that I agreed. I think she understood because she stopped talking about it. Instead she asked me why I had wanted to see her.

I pulled some papers out of my jacket pocket and placed them on the table. "I was hoping you could take a look at this."

"What is it?"

"Osamu Nonoguchi's account of what happened."

Rie Hidaka frowned, clearly displeased. "I'd rather not. I'm sure it's just a long list of the horrible things my husband did to him. Besides, I've already read what was in the papers."

"I believe you're talking about the confession Mr. Nonoguchi wrote after he was arrested. This is different. This is a falsified account he wrote after the crime in order to throw the police off his trail."

This she seemed to understand, though she still looked displeased. "Okay. But how can reading something that isn't true help?"

"I understand your confusion, but I'd really appreciate it if you could just take a look. It's not very long; you'll be able to finish it in no time."

"You want me to read it here?"

"If you would, yes."

She shook her head, but said nothing more. She picked up the pages and started to read. Fifteen minutes later, she looked up. "Okay. Now what?"

"Of the events recorded in this account, Mr. Nonoguchi has admitted that the description of his conversation with

Kunihiko Hidaka was fabricated. It wasn't as easygoing as he suggests, but a rather heated argument."

"So it seems."

"In addition, the description of events when he left your house is different than what really happened. Though you only showed him to the door, he claims in this account that you showed him to the gate."

"Right, we talked about that before."

"Is there anything else? Anything that differs from your memory of what happened?"

"Other than the sending off?" She looked confused for a moment, then scanned the account again. She shook her head. "No. I don't see anything."

"How about something Mr. Nonoguchi did or said on that day that isn't written here? Do you remember anything? Even a slight detail might be helpful. Such as whether or not he went to the bathroom."

"I don't remember precisely, but, no, I don't think he used the bathroom."

"Did you see or hear him make any phone calls while he was there?"

"Well, he could've called someone from my husband's office without me knowing."

To Rie Hidaka, it had been just another ordinary day at the time Nonoguchi dropped in. Of course she wouldn't remember every detail.

I was ready to give up when she suddenly looked up and said, "Actually, there was one thing."

"Yes?"

"I'm sure this has nothing to do with the case, though."

"Anything you can tell me might help."

"Well, that day, when Mr. Nonoguchi was leaving, he gave me a bottle of champagne. He said it was a present."

"Are you sure it happened that day?"

"Oh, absolutely sure."

"You say he gave it to you as he was leaving. Do remember the details of the exchange?"

"Well, it was after he came out of the office, just as Ms. Fujio was going in. It was in a paper bag, like it had just come from the store. He said he'd gotten so absorbed in talking to my husband that he'd forgotten to give it to him. He suggested my husband and I might drink it later that night at the hotel."

"And what did you do with it?"

"Well, I accepted it, of course, and brought it to the hotel. I left it in the hotel refrigerator. I never went back for it after what happened that night. The hotel even called me about it later, and I told them they could do whatever they wanted with it."

"So you didn't drink it?"

"By myself? No. I put it in there to chill so I could drink it with Kunihiko once he got to the hotel that night."

"Had Mr. Nonoguchi ever brought alcohol as a gift before?"

"As far as I'm aware, that was the only time. Mr. Nonoguchi doesn't drink."

"I see."

In his confession, Nonoguchi had written that he'd brought a bottle of scotch the first time he visited the Hidakas', but of course Rie hadn't been there at that time. I asked if she remembered anything else from the day that she couldn't find in the account. She thought about it long and hard, but ultimately told me that there was nothing else. Then she asked me why I was asking her about all this now.

"There's a lot of paperwork that needs to be done in order to close a case. This kind of fact-checking is just part of that process."

I don't think she doubted my explanation.

I concluded our interview, once again gave her my condolences, and left. Immediately after leaving the shopping center, I phoned the hotel where the Hidakas were supposed to have spent the night of his death and asked about the champagne. It took a while, but eventually they put me through to the manager who had been on duty at the time.

He spoke to me in the crisp, clear tones of a service-industry professional. "I believe it was a bottle of Dom Pérignon rosé. It was found in the room refrigerator. It's an expensive bottle and was unopened, so I called to inform the guest. She told me we should dispose of it as we saw fit, so I did."

I asked what he had done with the champagne, and after a bit of hesitation he told me that he'd taken it home. I then asked him whether he had drunk it.

He said that he had, two weeks earlier. He'd already thrown out the bottle. "Should I not have done that?"

"No, it's not a problem at all. Was the champagne good?"

"Oh, very."

I thanked him and hung up.

Back at home, I watched a copy, which I'd had forensics dupe for me, of the video of Osamu Nonoguchi sneaking into the Hidakas' house. I rewound and watched it several times, but my only reward was having that monotonous scene burned into my retinas over and over.

May 16
At slightly after one in the afternoon I arrived at the Yokoda Real Estate branch in Ikebukuro. The small office had two desks behind a counter with windows facing the street.

Inside, I found Miyako Fujio working alone. She informed me that everyone else was out with clients and she couldn't leave the office, so we sat at the table attached to the front counter and talked there. From the outside, it probably looked as though a shady-looking man had come in, hoping to find a cheap apartment.

I cut straight to the chase. "Are you familiar with the details of Nonoguchi's confession?"

She nodded, her face drawn taut. "I read what was in the papers."

"What did you think?"

"Well, nothing, except I was very surprised. I had no idea *Forbidden Hunting Grounds* was written by someone else."

"According to what Nonoguchi told us, Kunihiko Hidaka hadn't been able to talk to you about the novel in detail because it wasn't his work. Does that jibe with your own experience talking to him?"

"Honestly, I can't say. It's true that Mr. Hidaka always brushed me off without getting very deep into specifics, but that hardly proves anything."

"Does anything you might have discussed with Mr. Hidaka seem odd to you in retrospect?"

"Nothing that I can recall. But it's hard to say. I never

imagined Mr. Hidaka wasn't the real author, so there's a good chance I wouldn't have noticed anything out of the ordinary."

I couldn't blame her for that. "How about anything that makes more sense now that you know Osamu Nonoguchi was the author?"

"Again, it's hard to say. Mr. Nonoguchi also went to the same school as my brother, so it's certainly possible that he wrote that novel. It's not like I knew Mr. Hidaka all that well, for that matter."

I was on the verge of giving up hope of any new information from Ms. Fujio when she said, "Just, if it's true that Mr. Hidaka didn't write that novel . . . I don't know, I might have to read it again before I say anymore. You see, I'd been convinced that one of the characters in the book was modeled on Mr. Hidaka himself."

"How so? Can you describe the character to me?"

"Have you read the book?"

"I haven't, though I did look at an outline. One of the other detectives read it and wrote up a summary for the rest of us."

"Well, part of the book details the main character's middle-school days. The main character's very violent, pressuring his friends to join in his antics, and attacking anyone who doesn't toe the line. They'd call it bullying, nowadays. Anyway, his favorite victim is a classmate of his, a boy named Hamaoka. I always thought that boy was a stand-in for Mr. Hidaka."

"Why did you think that student was Mr. Hidaka?"

"Well, the book is written as if it were Hamaoka's own recollections. And since it's really more of a roman à clef than a work of pure fiction, it made sense that the narrator was actually the author—thus, Mr. Hidaka."

I nodded.

"Also," Miyako Fujio said, after a moment's hesitation, "it occurred to me that Mr. Hidaka wrote that novel for a specific reason."

I looked up at her. "What reason is that?"

"In the book, Hamaoka's hatred for the main character is obvious. You can feel it practically emanating from every page. Though it's never said outright in the book, you get the sense that it's this hatred that moves Hamaoka to investigate the eventual death of the man who bullied him in school. If Hamaoka's hatred was the author's hatred, well, it would make sense for Mr. Hidaka to have written his book as a way to get revenge on my brother. That's how I interpreted it, at least."

I stared at her. The idea of writing a book for revenge hadn't even occurred to me until she'd mentioned it. In fact, our investigative team hadn't paid much attention to *Forbidden Hunting Grounds* at all.

"So Nonoguchi's confession throws off your theory," I said.

"It does. But really, it doesn't matter whether it was Mr. Hidaka or Mr. Nonoguchi who wrote it. As long as the author was the model for that boy, it's all the same. Just . . . I've had the image of Hamaoka being Kunihiko Hidaka in my head for so long that it's hard for me to picture someone else in his place. Sort of like when your favorite book gets made into a TV show and the actor doesn't match your image of the character."

"So does Kunihiko Hidaka match the character of Hamaoka in your mind?"

"I think so . . . but that might just be because when I first read it, I assumed that character was him."

I asked her what she would do now that the author of *Forbidden Hunting Grounds* was Osamu Nonoguchi.

She thought for a moment, then said, her voice cold, "I'll wait until I hear the results of Mr. Nonoguchi's trial. Then I'll decide on an appropriate response."

When I got back to the precinct, the chief of detectives was waiting to speak to me. He called me into his office and wanted to know why I hadn't wrapped up this case and forwarded everything to the prosecutor's office. He wasn't too pleased when I told him I was still investigating the murder of Kunihiko Hidaka. I can hardly blame him for questioning the need to continue sniffing around when the murderer had already confessed in full, provided a compelling motive for his actions, which was backed by sufficient evidence, and even wrote his own confession.

"So, what doesn't fit?" he asked, his irritation plain. "From where I'm sitting, this looks pretty cut-and-dried."

I had no real basis to deny any of the evidence—the most vital pieces of which I had uncovered myself. Until recently, I, too, had felt that nothing was left to know about the murder of the bestselling author. I'd succeeded in breaking down Nonoguchi's false alibi and uncovering the truth behind his relationship with Hidaka. I was rather proud of what I'd accomplished.

But doubt had crept in around the edges of my assurance. It happened while I was writing up a report after questioning Nonoguchi in his hospital bed. My eyes strayed to his hand, down to his fingertips, and a sudden disturbing thought occurred to me. At the time, I decided to ignore it. It was too far-fetched, too unrealistic.

Yet I was unable to ignore the thought. It proved persistent, refusing eviction from the back corners of my mind. I should mention that, even when I first arrested Nonoguchi, I was apprehensive, afraid that I might have taken a wrong turn. Now that apprehension was becoming even more pointed.

Of course, it's entirely possible that my doubt is a delusion, more indicative of my shortcomings as a detective and a person than of any great undiscovered truth. Yet I'm unwilling to bring closure to this case while that doubt still lingers.

For what must've been the dozenth time, I carefully reread Osamu Nonoguchi's confession. As I did, I asked myself several questions that hadn't previously occurred to me:

1. If Kunihiko Hidaka was using Osamu Nonoguchi's murder attempt to blackmail him into being his ghostwriter, then, what would have happened if Nonoguchi decided to turn himself in and let the chips fall where they may? It would have done considerable damage to Hidaka as well. It might even have ruined his writing career. Why wasn't Hidaka afraid of this? According to Nonoguchi, he didn't turn himself in because he didn't want to involve Hatsumi, but Hidaka couldn't have known with any certainty Nonoguchi would react this way.

2. Why didn't Nonoguchi start to resist Hidaka's blackmail after Hatsumi's death? His account asserts that he'd grown tired of the constant psychological warfare. But, if that was the case, wouldn't that have made turning himself in an even more appealing option?

3. Would the videotape and the knife really have been sufficient evidence for an attempted murder charge? The only thing caught on tape was Nonoguchi going in through Hidaka's

office window, and no traces of blood were on the knife. Moreover, the only person at the scene other than the would-be murderer and intended victim was Hatsumi, a conspirator to murder. Depending on her testimony, it seemed to me that chances were good Nonoguchi would be found innocent if he was even brought to trial in the first place.

4. In his confession, Nonoguchi writes that his relationship with Hidaka became that of a genuine collaborator. Considering all that had passed before then, was that really possible?

I questioned Nonoguchi on these four points. He had one answer for all of them:

"You might think it's strange, but I can't change what happened just to suit you. I can't tell you why I did what I did when I did it. All I can say is, I wasn't in my right mind. Not for several years."

This left me with little to go on. If there were something concrete, a contradiction I could wave in his face, I might get somewhere. But my doubts were ethereal, psychological questions rather than cold, hard facts.

However, there was another reason for my misgivings, one that overshadowed all four of these points.

It comes down to character. I know the man Osamu Nonoguchi far better than the chief or any of the other investigators who worked on the case. And what I know about his character and what he claims in his confession just don't match up.

I have grown increasingly unwilling to abandon an alternative theory of mine, one that has arisen out of these doubts. A theory that, if correct, would explain everything.

I had a clear purpose in going to see Rie Hidaka. I was sure that, if my conjecture was correct, then Osamu Nonoguchi's first account of the discovery of her husband had an entirely different purpose from what I'd initially assumed.

I was, however, unable to elicit any useful information. The only new piece of information that I'd gleaned from her was that Nonoguchi had brought the Hidakas a bottle of champagne. Nonoguchi might simply have forgotten to mention this in his account. Or perhaps he left it out for some reason. It seemed meaningful, since he did not typically bring alcohol when he visited—though it might've simply been a send-off present for the couple's imminent move. If there was some other, deeper meaning, I didn't uncover it. Still, I filed the bottle of champagne away in my mind for possible future use.

I believe it's necessary to completely reassess the relationship between Osamu Nonoguchi and Kunihiko Hidaka. If I have indeed taken a wrong turn somewhere, then I need to go back to the beginning and start over.

To this end, it was useful meeting with Miyako Fujio. When I was talking with her, I realized what I needed to do next. To clarify the relationship between the two men, I'd have to go back to their days together in middle school. In researching this, the novel-cum-documentary *Forbidden Hunting Grounds* should prove an excellent resource.

After meeting with Ms. Fujio, I went straight to a bookstore and bought a copy of the book, which I started reading on the train home. It was a quick read, partly because I already knew how the story went. As usual, however, I am no judge of the novel's literary worth.

As Miyako Fujio had said, the book was written from the viewpoint of the character Hamaoka. The story begins with Hamaoka, an employee at a nondescript company, reading in the morning paper about the stabbing death of a woodblock artist. Hamaoka recalls that this woodblock artist, Kazuya Nishina, was the ringleader of a group of bullies who used to torment Hamaoka in middle school. The book then slides into an account of the bullying he endured.

The bullying comes to a peak during Hamaoka's last year in middle school, when he gets beaten up several times— thrashed within an inch of his life. On one occasion he is stripped, wrapped in cellophane, and abandoned in a corner of the gymnasium. On another he's walking beneath a window and a cup of hydrochloric acid is emptied on his head. He gets beaten up in more "traditional" ways as well. Verbal abuse and mean-spirited pranks are part of his daily life.

The account was meticulously detailed, the descriptions designed for maximum impact. I could understand why Miyako Fujio called it more journalism than fiction.

But why Hamaoka becomes the target of so much abuse is never made clear. He claims it just started one day, as though he had "stepped on the wrong grave and angered an evil spirit." In this account, I saw similarities to other bullying incidents that I was aware from my time as a teacher. At first, the target tries to keep his head up, but he eventually succumbs to fear and depression.

"What was most frightening was not the violence itself, but the negative energy emitted by those other boys who hated him. He had never imagined that such malice existed in the world."

I feel this line from *Forbidden Hunting Grounds* is an honest portrayal of the victim's feelings. When I was a teacher, I

found that victims of bullying were often bewildered at what
seemed like the sheer arbitrariness of the attacks.

Fortunately for Hamaoka, the bullying stopped when
the ringleader suddenly transferred to another school. No one
knew where Nishina had gone, but it was rumored that he'd
been sent away because he attacked a girl.

The story then moves beyond Hamaoka's middle-school
days. After a few twists and turns in the plot (which seemed
unrelated to the case at hand), Hamaoka begins trying to follow Kazuya Nishina's trail.

The remainder of the book is divided between Hamaoka's
recollections and the results of his investigation. The first thing
the reader learns is the truth behind Nishina's departure from
Hamaoka's school. The girl he attacked was a student at a
nearby all-girls Catholic middle school. Nishina had his cronies
hold her down, raped her in plain sight, and filmed the whole
thing. He'd intended to sell the film to a local gang, who would
distribute it. None of this made it into the papers because the
parents of the girl were well connected and wanted to keep
the incident under wraps.

This revelation concludes the first half of the book, which
is largely concerned with Kazuya Nishina's cruelty. The second half of the book talks about the sudden change in his life
after he develops an interest in woodblock printing and de-
cides to become an artist. The story ends when, just before his
first gallery show, a prostitute approaches him on the street
and stabs him to death. It's common knowledge that the stabbing was based on fact.

I could see how Miyako Fujio would assume that Hamaoka

was a fictional stand-in for the author. If this were a typical novel, that would be a foolish assumption. In the case of a work so closely based on actual events, it seemed the most likely explanation.

Her theory that the author had written the book to get revenge on his tormentor also had merit. As she asserted, the portrayal of Kazuya Nishina was anything but favorable throughout the book. One could imagine a gentler telling of the story of a troubled youth who becomes an artist, one that didn't go into such emphatic detail about the man's ugliness and moral weakness. This was probably the reasoning behind Miyako Fujio's claim that her family name was being dragged through the mud.

Yet if we assumed Hamaoka was a stand-in for Osamu Nonoguchi, something was missing: Where was Kunihiko Hidaka in the story? (Or, if Hidaka was the author, we'd have to ask, where was Nonoguchi?)

The book is ostensibly a work of fiction. Characters may have been written out. But that wasn't what bugged me. If, as the novel suggested, Osamu Nonoguchi had been bullied during middle school, I wondered what Kunihiko Hidaka had done about it at the time. Was he sitting by silently, letting it all happen?

I persist in this line of inquiry for one reason: in his account of the events surrounding the murder, Nonoguchi repeatedly refers to Kunihiko Hidaka as his "friend."

It is unfortunate, but true, that parental guidance and the intervention of teachers often has little effect in bullying cases. Friendship is a child's greatest ally. Yet if the character of Hamaoka had any friends, they didn't get involved.

And a friend who lets his friend get bullied isn't a friend at all.

The same contradiction was apparent in Osamu Nonoguchi's confession. Friends don't steal friends' wives. Friends don't conspire with said wives to kill their friends. And friends don't blackmail friends into becoming their ghostwriters.

So why did Nonoguchi ever consider Kunihiko Hidaka his friend?

It was all explained by the new theory I was working on—the theory that came to me the moment I saw the pen callus on the side of Osamu Nonoguchi's middle finger.

7
THE PAST (PART TWO)

OLD ACQUAINTANCES—KAGA'S
INTERVIEWS

Interview: Junichi Hayashida

I'm not really sure I can tell you anything useful—middle school was an awful long time ago! Twentysome-odd years, right? My memory's pretty good, but that's ancient history.

On Hidaka:

To be totally honest with you, I didn't even know there was an author named Kunihiko Hidaka until a couple of weeks ago. I haven't read a novel in years. I know I should read more—I'm a barber and it's good to be able to talk with the customers about the latest stuff—but I just can't find the time. Anyway, it was only when I read about what happened in the newspapers that I found out about Hidaka. I do read the newspaper, at least. I wouldn't have even realized he was my classmate if they hadn't done that special bit on Nonoguchi's and Hidaka's past. Yeah, that was a surprise, finding out I went to school with a bestselling author and a murderer both!

On Nonoguchi:

I remember Gooch, a lot better than the other guy. I don't think Hidaka stood out that much; he was one of those people who don't really make an impression on you. I had no idea they were friends, either.

"Gooch"? Yeah, that's what we called him. I don't know

why, it just kinda fit. He was sort of slow—just kind of a gooch. He was always reading, though. We sat next to each other in class for a while, that's why I remember. No idea what he was reading. I wasn't all that interested in reading back then either, I guess. I just know it wasn't comic books. He was great in composition class, too. Our homeroom teacher taught composition, actually, so he was always kind of a teacher's pet.

On bullying:

Yeah, there was some of that. They talk about bullying a lot in the news lately, but it was always around. And people who say it wasn't as mean back then are full of it. I mean, being mean is the point, right?

And Gooch, he spent his share of time in the crosshairs. Actually, yeah, he got beat up pretty bad. People messing with his lunchbox, taking his money. He probably got locked in the janitor's closet once or twice, too. He was just the type, the kind bullies like to pick on.

The cellophane-wrap incident:

You mean they wrapped him up in that stuff they use in the kitchen? Yeah, maybe I heard about something along those lines. But you gotta understand, there were things like that going on all the time.

The hydrochloric acid incident:

I didn't hear about that, but it could've happened. It wasn't the best middle school, to say the least. Mayhem was pretty much par for the course.

Were you ever involved?

Well, it's nothing I'm proud of, but, yeah, I knocked some heads together once or twice. Just a little, though. Nothing serious. Honestly. See, the problem kids liked getting us regular students involved. If you resisted, you'd be the next one on the chopping block, so you kind of had to go along with 'em. It felt terrible. I mean, who wants to beat up on some snot-nosed little kid who doesn't even fight back? Everyone knew it was going on, too. I remember I put some dog shit in this kid's bag once, and our student leader was sitting right there, but she pretended not to see. Masuoka, her name was. Even if you weren't helping 'em, you were letting 'em get away with it. Yeah, those kids loved picking on people, but I think they liked getting us other students' hands dirty even more. Of course, I didn't think about it like that back then.

On Fujio:

Oh, yeah, no way I could forget Fujio. I don't think I was the only one who wished he'd disappear. I bet even the teachers were hoping he'd walk off a cliff.

He was just a bad egg. He thought nothing of making some poor kid's life a living hell. He was bigger than some of the grown-ups, too, and really strong, so who was going to stop him? Course, when the other bullies figured that out, they fell all over each other to be friends with him. Figured they were safer being on the winning side. I think that just encouraged him, you know? Fujio's the kind of kid they're talking about when they say someone's a lost cause.

Was Fujio the ringleader?

Oh, yeah, without a doubt. He called all the shots. I even heard that whenever any of the kids in his posse stole someone's lunch money, they had to give it to him first, and he would distribute it. Basically no different from the yakuza, really.

On Fujio's departure:

Boy, were we happy when he left school. I mean, peace at

last, finally! Things did change a lot after he left, too. It was like a big mood shift. There were still a few bad seeds around, but it was nothing like when Fujio was in charge. I didn't ever find out what happened to him, though. There was a rumor he'd beat up some kid from another school and got sent to juvie, but I doubt it was anything as big as that, or it probably would've made the local paper.

Does Fujio have something to do with your case, Detective? Didn't Nonoguchi kill Hidaka because he was stealing his books?

The other members of Fujio's circle:

No idea what became of them. They're probably all productive members of society.

I think I've got a class roster around here somewhere. The addresses and phone numbers are old, though. Hang on, I'll go get it. . . .

Interview: Harumi Nitta

Mr. Hayashida gave you my name? Junichi Hayashida? I don't even remember a Hayashida in my class. No . . . No, I'm sure he was there. I've just kind of blocked the whole thing out, I guess.

So, where to begin? My maiden name was Masuoka, and, yes, I was a student leader. They picked one boy and one girl every year. It's not like we had any real responsibilities. We mostly just made sure everyone got their homework assignments and delivered messages for the teacher. Oh, and we helped run student meetings in homeroom. Boy, there's a word I haven't used in years. I don't have any kids.

On Hidaka and Nonoguchi:

I'm really sorry, but I hardly remember either of them. I

mostly hung out with the girls. That's just how it is in middle school.

On bullying:

There was probably some bullying going on with the boys, but I never noticed anything. It's hard to say what I would've done if I had noticed, but probably telling the teacher would've been a good place to start.

I'm sorry, but . . . my husband will be home any minute. If you've got what you need, can we wrap this up? I really don't think I know anything that'd be of any help. Also, I'd really appreciate it if you didn't tell anyone else I went to that middle school. It's just . . . a difficult subject. I haven't even told my husband. Thanks.

Interview: Masatoshi Tsuburaya

Thanks for coming out here. Why not come inside? Sure . . . we can talk right here in the hall, if you prefer.

On Hidaka and Nonoguchi:

Oh, I remember them, sure. I've been retired, let's see . . . about ten years, but I remember every single one of the students in my classes. You spend that much time with the same kids for a whole year, you get to know them pretty well. And those two were in my first class after I started teaching at that school. You don't forget your first bunch of students.

Nonoguchi, he was a star in composition. He might not have gotten 100 on every paper, but he was right up there. As for Hidaka, no, he didn't leave too much of an impression on me in terms of his schoolwork. Good or bad.

On bullying:

I don't think Hidaka got bullied much, and Nonoguchi

definitely didn't. There were some bad kids, sure, but I never heard about anything happening to him.

Hayashida said he was bullied. . . .

Well, that comes as a real surprise! I certainly had no idea. And don't give me that detective look, that's the honest truth. There wouldn't be any point lying about it now, would there?

Look, the reason why I said Nonoguchi definitely wasn't bullied is because, if anything, he was on the other side of the equation. He had this phase where he was hanging out with the bad kids; it got to the point where I was pretty worried about him. His parents even came in to talk to me about it. I seem to recall talking to him about all of this on occasion.

Of course when a kid starts hanging out with the wrong crowd, there isn't much that's going to save him if he doesn't have an ally. I don't mean me, or any other teacher, or his parents. It was his friend Hidaka that turned him around. You wouldn't know it to look at him, but that Hidaka was a tough cookie. He couldn't stand to see people getting stepped on. He'd even lay into us teachers sometimes if he felt like we were being too hard on the class.

I think it was around New Year's when those two boys came to my house to visit. It was more like Hidaka brought Nonoguchi along with him. They didn't say much, but I got the feeling that they were there to apologize for giving me grief at school.

I was sure the two of them would go on to be best friends for life, so it was a bit of a shock when they ended up going off to different high schools. They both did pretty well in their classes, so I wouldn't think they'd have had any trouble getting into the same place if they'd wanted to.

It's really a shame what happened. I wonder what went wrong along the way. I wouldn't have expected that of either of them.

Interview: Tomoyo Hirosawa
The Nonoguchi boy? Sure, I remember him. They were our neighbors. He came by every once in a while to buy bread. We had a shop, up until about ten years ago.

On the murder:

Now that was a surprise. I mean, those boys? Doing those things? It's enough to make you wonder.

On Nonoguchi's childhood:

Well . . . I don't mean to speak ill of him, but little Osamu had a . . . dark side, you might say. Kinda like he was too grown-up sometimes, maybe even a little depressed.

I think it was back in elementary school, but there was a while when he didn't even go to school. I saw him up on the second floor of his house one day, and I called up to him.

"Hey there, Osamu. Are you sick? Do you have a cold?"

But, Detective, he didn't even answer. A little boy like that! He just pulled his head back inside and shut the curtains. It was a little creepy, to be honest. When you'd see him on the street, he'd always walk way off to one side and never look you in the eyes.

I heard later from a friend that there was a stretch where he didn't go to school at all. I don't know the reason why, but everyone said it was the parents' fault. They were both regular working people, nice enough, but I think they both felt like they deserved more. You know how people are sometimes. And they were overprotective of that boy! I remember the mother saying something about wanting to send him to some private elementary school. "We don't have the connections," she told me, "so Osamu's slumming it at the local school."

I never! *Slumming* it? My daughter and son both went to that school and they turned out fine, thank you very much.

That family never did fit in, though. I think they only moved here because of Mr. Nonoguchi's work. They must have come from some pretty fancy neighborhood if they thought our town wasn't up to snuff.

Anyway, it's not hard to see why their boy wouldn't want to go to school, what with his parents saying things like that. The apple doesn't fall far from the tree and all that. Of course, they got worried when he stopped going altogether. Not that you ever saw them dragging him back to school.

I think the only reason he ended up going again was thanks to Kunihiko. That's right, the Hidakas' boy. The one who got killed. Kunihiko used to drop by Osamu's house every morning to walk with him to school. I don't know who arranged it, but since they were in the same year, maybe one of the teachers put him up to it.

I'd see them every morning. First Kunihiko would pass by the house, and he'd always say hello to me in a nice big voice. That's a good kid right there, I'd say to myself. Then I'd see him walking back the other direction with Osamu in tow. It was funny, 'cause Kunihiko would always say hi again, but you wouldn't hear a peep out of Osamu. He'd just be there, walking along, looking down at the ground. Every day.

I guess that's what got Osamu going to school more regularly, though. Seeing as how he made it all the way to college,

I'd say he owed Kunihiko a debt. Course after what happened . . . It's enough to make you wonder.

Were they friends?

I saw them play together quite a bit. They used to hang out with the boy from the futon shop. I'm pretty sure it was Kunihiko initiating things, though, as always. But they got along pretty well.

Kunihiko wasn't just nice to Osamu, you know. He was nice to all the kids, especially the little ones. That's part of the reason why I have real trouble believing what happened.

Interview: Yukio Matsushima

Well, I don't know what to say. I nearly fell down when I heard the news. Just hearing those names brings me way back. It's true, I played with them quite a bit back in elementary school. My parents ran a futon shop, and we always used to get in trouble, jumping on the new futons back in the warehouse.

But, to tell you the truth, we weren't like best buddies or anything. It was more that there just weren't any other kids our age in the neighborhood to play with. Toward the end of elementary school, I started hanging out more with my other friends, even the ones who lived farther away.

On Osamu and Nonoguchi's relationship:

Well, I wouldn't exactly describe them as the best of friends either. I'm not sure what you'd call them.

Mrs. Hirosawa, the baker on your street, said they were friends.

Well, that just goes to show you how little adults understand about kids.

The thing is, theirs wasn't what you'd call an "equal relationship." Hidaka was always on top. I think things just sort of happened that way after he helped Nonoguchi out at school. He didn't lord it over him or anything, but you could tell by the way they acted. Hidaka was always the leader, Nonoguchi was always following. We used to go frog catching quite a bit, and it would always be Hidaka telling Nonoguchi what to do. That spot's dangerous, or find some better footing before you grab 'em, or take off your shoes. It wasn't like he was giving him orders. He was more like a mother hen, just flapping his wings. Kind of like a big brother, even though they were the same age.

Of course, I don't think Nonoguchi appreciated it all that much. He'd say things behind Hidaka's back. Never to his face, though.

In fact, I'm pretty sure that around the time I stopped playing with them, they stopped playing with each other, too. Part of the reason was Nonoguchi started going to an after-school program. That kind of cuts down on the playtime. But I also think Nonoguchi's mom didn't like the Hidakas. I overheard her once talking to him about them. "I hope you're not playing with that boy anymore!" she said, and she sounded pretty mean. The look on her face was enough to give you nightmares. It didn't make much sense to me as a kid. Why couldn't he play with Hidaka if he wanted to? What was wrong with his family? Even today I'm not sure why she said that.

On Nonoguchi's truancy:

Well, I don't know for sure, but maybe it was just that school didn't suit him. I don't think he ever had many friends. I remember him saying something about transferring to another school, a better one. But that never happened, and he stopped talking about it after a while.

That's about all I have for you. Sorry I don't remember more, but it was a couple of decades ago after all.

On the murder:

What do you want me to say? I was surprised. I mean, I only knew them as kids, so I obviously don't have the whole story, but it's not what I would've expected. At least, not the part about Hidaka using him as a ghostwriter. He might have been a bit overbearing with the kid, but he never pushed him around. And he had a real sense of justice, Hidaka did. Of course, people do change, and usually not for the better.

Interview: Junji Takahashi

Let me just say, never in a million years did I expect a detective to come down here and question me about this. I mean, I barely remembered those two till I read about 'em in the paper. We weren't close or nothing, so what's it got to do with me, right? And that whole ghostwriting thing, yeah, well, me and literature are about as far apart as you can get and still be on the same planet, and we got no plans of getting closer. (Laughs)

On middle school:

Man, I've been trying to forget that place ever since I got out of it! So Hayashida told you about me? He never did know when to shut up. (Laughs)

On bullying:

They talk about it like it's some big social problem these days, but whatever. Yeah, I gave a few wedgies in my day. (Laughs) I mean, we were just kids, right? And the way I see it, you need a bit of that when you're a kid. Not that I'm trying to make excuses or anything, but think about it: Once you grow up and get out there in the real world, there's all kinds of bad things waiting for you, right? So school is like practice for all that. You make it through the tough stuff, and you get a little stronger, a little wiser. That's what I think. They make such a big deal out of it these days, man. It's just kids being kids.

If you really want to know about what happened back then, there's a much better way than talking to me. Hey, I don't mind talking about it, but I've forgotten a bunch, and it's hard to keep it all straight sometimes. Hell, I lose track of what I'm saying when I'm trying to talk about something that happened yesterday! (Laughs)

So, right, it's much better if you just read that book, the one out under Hidaka's name. What was it called? *Forbidden hunter* or something?

Forbidden Hunting Grounds?

Yeah, that was it. You heard about that one, Detective? Well, then you could've saved yourself the trouble coming out here to talk to me.

Anyway, I don't read books at all, but when I heard about the murder, I thought I might take a peak at that one. That was my first time ever in the library. I almost got nervous just walking in there, like I was going to get in trouble or something. (Laughs)

So, right, I read that book because when I heard about it, especially the part about Fujio being the model for one of the characters, it sounded like it was pretty much our middle school. So I thought, hey, maybe I show up in there, too.

You read it, Detective?

Right, well, don't tell anyone else this, but it's all true. No, seriously. It might be written up like it's a novel and stuff, but everything in there's the stone-cold truth, no frills. Course all the names are changed. But everything else is exactly like it happened. Read that, and you'll know it all. It's got stuff in there even I forgot.

You remember the bit about the kid getting wrapped in cellophane and dumped in the gym? Man, when I read that, I started sweating bullets. (Laughs) See, I was the one in charge of that whole thing. It's not like I'm proud about it. But, you know, a kid's gotta blow off steam somehow, right?

Anyway, it was Fujio calling all the shots. He didn't do much himself, not directly, but he gave the orders. It wasn't like he was our leader or nothing, but if you ran with his crew, you were guaranteed a good time. So we did. (Laughs)

On the rape:

I don't know much about that. No, for real. I knew he had his eye on some girl. Long hair, kinda short, pretty girl. Fujio was big as a gorilla, but he had a thing for the real little ones, that was his type. That's all in the book, too. I was pretty impressed when I read that. The writer really knew his stuff. Of course, it makes sense if it was Gooch writing it.

Then there's that bit about Fujio disappearing every once in a while? I think in the book, he keeps stepping out right during the middle of sixth period, I mean before school was even finished. But that's not exactly right. He didn't leave in the middle of sixth period, he'd leave right when it was done. That's why he was never in homeroom at the end of the day. As for where he was going, the book got *that* right. There was a street that pretty little girl always walked home along, and that's where he'd go. But he never brought any of us with him.

He went alone. So I can't really say what he was up to. Except, I bet what the book says is close enough. I can totally imagine him hiding behind some tree, checking her out, laying his plans. Kinda creepy when you think about it, right? (Laughs)

Except, when he did that thing to the girl, he wasn't alone. He brought someone with him. I don't know who. No, for real. I'm not trying to protect anyone. Why would I? It wasn't me! Look, I did some bad things, but I'm not helping anyone rape someone. You gotta believe me.

It was only one other person?

I know what the book says, about the guys keeping a lookout and the videotape and all, but that's not how it went down. There was just one other kid, the guy holding her down. And it wasn't a videotape, it was just a picture. Taken with a Polaroid camera. Fujio took the picture himself, the way I heard it. I don't know what happened to it though. I'm pretty sure that bit about Fujio selling the tape to the yakuza was all made up, too. I never saw the picture, at any rate. (Laughs) I wanted to at the time, though, sorry to say. But it never got as far as me.

Actually, you know who might know something? Nakatsuka. He was like Fujio's right-hand man, and Fujio used to give him stuff to hold on to, you know, in case the cops ever searched him. (Laughs) If Fujio gave that photo to anyone, it would have been Nakatsuka. Course I doubt he'd still have it.

I don't have his contact info here, but his first name was Akio. Akio Nakatsuka.

Didn't Nonoguchi tell you anything about all this? I'm pretty sure he knows most of it. That's how he wrote that book, right? Maybe it's not the easiest stuff to talk about, but still.

Why is it hard to talk about?

Well, come on. Who wants to drag lousy stuff that happened to them when they were a kid out into the light? Most people bury it and move on.

Was Nonoguchi bullied?

Gooch? Sure, but not for long. Fujio never took him seriously, not at first. No, he had his eye on Hidaka. Thought that kid was too big for his own britches. He pulled out all the stops, really gave him a thrashing, but Hidaka never flinched. So Fujio just kept getting worse, trying to put the little punk in his place, you know? And that's how it escalated to that stuff in the book.

Hidaka was the victim?

That's right. It was Hidaka we wrapped up in that cellophane. Pretty sure the acid out the window was meant for him, too.

Not Nonoguchi?

Oh, no, by then Gooch was with us, totally. One of the guys. He was the closest thing to an underling Fujio ever had. We used to send him on errands, and stuff like that.

Weren't Hidaka and Nonoguchi friends?

Hardly. Well, I don't know what happened after they graduated, of course. They come across as best buddies in all the newspaper reports, but that must've been after middle school, because it certainly wasn't true back when I knew them. I mean, Nonoguchi used to rat out Hidaka to Fujio all the time, telling him things Hidaka was saying behind his back. If it weren't for that, I doubt Fujio would've been so gung ho about showing Hidaka who was boss.

On the character Hamaoka:

Oh, yeah, that was Hidaka. No doubt about it. I know

Nonoguchi wrote the book, but since he had to do it in Hidaka's name, maybe that's why he made him the main character?

Which character in the book was Nonoguchi?

Huh, kinda hard to say. Just one of the bullies, I guess.

Course, that doesn't make a whole lot of sense, does it? A bully publishing a book under his victim's name? What's up with that?

Interview: Koichi Mitani

I'd appreciate it if we can keep this short. I've got a meeting to get to.

I'm not even really sure what it is you expect to learn from talking to me. I know you detectives have to scour every bit of your suspect's past, but the last time I knew Nonoguchi was when we were in high school!

I've spoken to his elementary school friends as well.

Wow, you're going that far back? Well, I don't know what to say about that. I suppose I wonder if it's really necessary. Not that I'm telling you how to do your job. (Laughs)

So . . . Nonoguchi was a pretty normal high school student, nothing special. We talked a lot, mostly because we liked the same books and movies and stuff like that.

Did he ever talk about becoming an author?

Oh, sure, he told me that was his ambition. I remember him writing some short stories in his notebooks and showing them to me. I don't remember most of them, but he wrote a lot of science fiction, as I recall. The stories were pretty good. At least good enough to entertain a high school student.

On Nonoguchi's choice of high school:

I don't know. I think it was probably just because his

grades in middle school were the right level for admission to our high school?

Wait, actually, now that you mention it, he did say something once about another high school that was closer to his house that he could've gone to, but he didn't want to for some reason.

Did he say why?

I think it had less to do with the school itself, and more to do with the neighborhood. He seemed really down on the whole place.

Did he mention his middle school?

Only that the people there were low class. Can you believe it? Low-class town, low-class school, low-class students— stuff like that. He was pretty cool normally, but whenever he'd talk about where he was from, he'd get all worked up. I clearly remember getting sick of it, so he must have talked about it more than once. Yeah, he was pretty strange back then. Most people think the town they grew up in is the best, right?

I think he felt like he'd gotten a bad deal because his father had to move there for work. He used to tell me he was only there temporarily, which is why he didn't really know anyone in the neighborhood and didn't play with any of the kids there. Of course, I didn't care about any of it. It was him telling me all this. Like he was making excuses for something. Besides, he didn't move away after all, at least not when I knew him.

There was another thing, too. . . . I think at one point he tried to switch elementary schools, but it didn't work out for some reason. He told me they wouldn't let him switch *because* he was going to school every day. He thought that was pretty ironic, "suffering through that hell day in and day out, and then getting punished for it." He said there was this kid, one of his neighbors, who used to come and pick him up every morning to walk to school together, which he couldn't stand. Like it was all some big neighborhood conspiracy to drag him down, right?

I remember thinking, I wish someone would come over and get me to go to school every morning! Talk about nice. But Nonoguchi was always Nonoguchi.

Was Hidaka the boy that walked to school with him?

He never said. In fact, he never mentioned Kunihiko Hidaka at all. This whole thing in the news was the first time I ever heard about him.

On Hidaka's novels:

Actually, I hadn't read any of them. I do read, but mostly mysteries. Light stuff, like those travel mysteries where they're going off someplace and somebody gets killed, you know those? I tend to stay away from the backbreaking stuff. If you have to work to get through a book, it's not very relaxing, is it?

Anyway, when I heard about the murder, I did pick one of them up. Sent chills down my spine to think that Nonoguchi was the author.

Which book?

Sea Ghost. The one about the artist whose wife cheats on him? It made sense in a lot of ways.

How so?

I mean, you could tell Nonoguchi wrote it. It just felt like him, you know? It was like his personality was stamped on every page. That stuff doesn't change from when you're a kid.

Actually, Hidaka wrote *Sea Ghost.*

What, really? Shows you how much I know! Guess I'd better stick with the light stuff. (Laughs)

Sorry, I've got to get to that meeting.

Interview: Yasushi Fujimura

Yes, I'm Osamu's uncle. Osamu's mother was my sister.

And as for our request for the profits from those books, it's not like we're just mindlessly clamoring for money. Frankly that's insulting. We just think things should be put right, that the air needs to be cleared. That's all we're saying.

But Osamu did murder Mr. Hidaka.

Of course, and he should be punished for it. He needs to pay his debt to society, and I think that was Osamu's intention when he confessed.

That only makes it more important that everything's on the table, you understand. It was a terrible thing he did, certainly, but he didn't do it without reason. It's important to think about his relationship with Mr. Hidaka, isn't it? This ghost-writer thing—he was writing those novels for Mr. Hidaka until the day he just couldn't take it anymore. That's what everyone—all the authorities—are saying.

In other words, some blame rests at the feet of Mr. Hidaka. It's not just Osamu who's in the wrong here. Why should Osamu be the only one punished? What about Mr. Hidaka's part in all this?

I don't know much about the literary market, but I hear that Kunihiko Hidaka's novels sold quite well. He was one of the top-ten highest earners, I hear. But who really earned that money? Wasn't he selling novels Osamu had written? Does it make sense for only Osamu to be punished, while the money he earned remains in someone else's hands? I don't think it does. If it were me, I would return that money. It's only fair.

I'm not sure the bereaved family agrees.

Oh, I'm sure they don't. That's why we're bringing in lawyers to get everything straight. I'm just trying to help Osamu out here. I don't want the money. It wouldn't be my money, anyway. It would go to Osamu.

But isn't this a matter for civil court, Detective?

Actually, I wanted to talk to you about your sister, and the neighborhood where her family lived.

Oh . . . so you didn't come here about the royalties? Right, well, my sister moved to that area shortly after Osamu was born. Built herself a house. Her husband's relatives sold them some land cheap, which is why they ended up in that particular spot.

Did she like it there?

Not much, no. She told me once that, had she known what sort of place it was beforehand, she never would've built there.

What didn't she like about it, specifically?

That, I'm not sure. I sort of avoided the subject. Speaking of which, why do you ask, Detective? Does this really have anything to do with the case? I understand you have a job to do, but worrying about my sister's choice of neighborhoods seems like stretching it a bit far!

Not that we have anything to hide.

Interview: Akio Nakatsuka

Nonoguchi? I've never heard of any Nonoguchi.

He was your classmate in middle school.

Really? Okay, like I'd remember *that.*

On the murder:

Sorry, haven't picked up a paper in a while. And I don't know anything about any authors.

He was your classmate, too.

Well, whaddya know. So, Detective, what's this have to do with me? I'm between jobs right now, and I kind of have to get down to the employment center, so I don't have a lot of time.

Do you remember anyone named Hidaka?

What? Yeah, I remember a Hidaka. He's the one who got offed? No kidding. Guess you never know how someone's going to check out till it happens.

So how's asking about his school going to help your investigation? Didn't you just say you already know who killed him? What's left to find out?

We're just making sure we have all the facts.

Things must be pretty quiet for you to be checking things after the murder's already solved!

On bullying:

Oh, c'mon. You don't think I—

Fine, yeah, I knocked Hidaka around a couple of times. Never for any particular reason. Just keeping him in his place, you know.

But that Hidaka, he was one tough cookie. I don't think we ever got money out of him. Most of those kids, you put the fear into them and they'll give you a thousand, two thousand yen just like that. So, yeah, we paid Hidaka special attention. Looking back at it, the kid had guts. Course at the time it just pissed us off.

On Nonoguchi:

Look, man, I told you I don't know any Nonoguchi . . .
wait, unless you mean the Gooch? Yeah, that's right, his name
was Nonoguchi, wasn't it. I remember him. He was Fujio's
moneybags.

You know, the thing you carry money in? Whenever
Fujio needed some cash, the Gooch was good for it. And he
had him running errands all the time. Man, what a wimp that
guy was.

Do you know what happened after Fujio left your school?

No, we all split up after that. I didn't see the Gooch very
much after that either.

On the assault:

Yeah, I heard about it, that girl from the Catholic school,
right? But I don't know much. That's the truth. Me and Fujio
were close, but he never told me stuff like that. And I hardly
ever saw him after he left. They had him grounded for months.

You weren't with him at the assault?

No way, man. I heard someone was there, but it sure
wasn't me. What does all this old crap have to do with your
case, anyway?

Look, I can tell you one thing. You said that Hidaka guy
was the one who got killed, right? I might not have seen Fujio
after he left, but I did see him—Hidaka—once, just about
three or four years ago. He came over to my place, said he
wanted to know about Fujio and the assault.

He told me he was writing a novel about Fujio. Can you
believe it? I didn't take him too seriously, so I didn't think
much about it. I guess if it became this big seller, I shoulda
asked for more money! (Laughs)

What did you tell him?

Just what I knew. He didn't seem like he held anything against me in particular, so what's the harm?

What exactly did you know?

Hardly anything. But he was persistent, wanted to know if I remembered any detail at all. Turns out he thought I was the one with Fujio, too.

On the photograph:

I don't know anything about a photograph.

I heard you might have it.

Who would say something like that? That's crazy.

Okay, okay . . . maybe Fujio did give me one, just before they got him. It was blurry as hell.

You kept it?

Yeah, what's the harm in that? Doesn't mean I did anything. It's not like I was holding on to it special or anything, either. I just forgot to throw it out. I bet if I searched your house, I'd find a few photos from when you were a kid, Detective.

Do you still have the photo?

No way. I threw it out a little while after Hidaka visited.

Did you show it to him?

Yeah, I showed it to him. I figured I owed him that much at least, what with our past, and him coming all the way out to see me. He wanted to borrow it, so I let him have it for a while. He sent it back a few days later in an envelope, though, with a note about him not believing in saving photographs or something. I just threw the thing in the trash, envelope and all.

Did you see Hidaka after that?

Nope.

Were there any other photographs?

Just the one. I don't know if Fujio even took any more photos than the one.

We done here?

Interview: Heikichi Tsujimura

Note: For this interview, I spoke with Mr. Tsujimura's granddaughter, who acted as his interpreter, since Mr. Tsujimura has difficulty speaking clearly.

How old is your grandfather?

Um, ninety-one, I think. His heart's strong, but he can't walk around anymore. Still sharp as a tack though, if a little hard of hearing.

When did he retire?

He stopped making fireworks about fifteen years ago. It was less his age and more a problem of supply and demand. They stopped doing fireworks shows down by the river so work got really slow. We think it was probably good timing, though. And since my father wasn't in the business, we didn't feel there was any need to keep it going.

Have you seen this book?

An Unburning Flame? Oh, it's by Kunihiko Hidaka! No, I hadn't heard of it. I don't think anyone in my family's read it.

Could you ask your grandfather?

I'll try, though I'm pretty sure I know the answer.

. . . No, he's never heard of it either. He hasn't read a book in years. What about it?

It's based on your grandfather's work.

Really? It's about a fireworks maker?

. . . Grandpa says that's a strange thing to write a book

about. Not many people know much about his line of work, he says.

On Hidaka's visits:

Really? Well, Grandpa used to have his workshop right next to the shrine in town. So Mr. Hidaka saw my grandfather work when he was a kid and wrote his novel about it?

. . . Grandpa says some of the neighborhood kids would come and play nearby sometimes. He tried to keep them away because it was dangerous, but some of them were persistent so he let them inside once or twice.

Were there many of these kids?

. . . Actually not that many, he says. He just remembers one.

Does he remember a name?

. . . Sorry, no. He says he didn't forget it, he never knew it in the first place.

Would he recognize the boy from a picture?

I'm not sure . . . it was a long time ago. I'll ask him, though.

. . . Okay, well, he says he remembers what the boy looked like. Do you have a photograph with you? Okay, let's show it to him.

. . . He says the boy he remembers was smaller than any of these kids. What is this? A middle-school yearbook? So the boy is one of the ones in this group here? But wouldn't he have been younger than this when he visited the workshop? Right, that's what I thought. Okay, well, I'll try to explain it to him. . . .

8

THE PAST (PART THREE)

KYOICHIRO KAGA'S STORY

I believe I've met with everyone I can who has anything notable to contribute about Osamu Nonoguchi's and Kunihiko Hidaka's past, particularly their time in middle school. I'm sure there are others I haven't been able to track down, but I feel I've obtained all I need for now. Though the evidence and testimony add up to something like a box of un-assembled jigsaw-puzzle pieces at the moment, I do have at least an idea of the completed picture in my mind, a picture that I believe reveals the full truth behind this case.

At the heart of everything is the bullying that took place during Nonoguchi's and Hidaka's middle school years, and which defined their future relationship. Once I realized the significance of those events, several other parts of the story fell into place. I'm now convinced that it is impossible to understand what happened on the day Hidaka died without first understanding this troubled history.

I know something about bullying, though not firsthand (as either victim or aggressor—at least, not so far as I'm aware). My experience is secondhand. Over ten years ago, I was a home-room teacher at a middle school, in charge of a class of ninth-graders.

Toward the end of the first semester the first signs appeared.

The semester-end exams provided the first clue: according to an English instructor, five of the students from homeroom had given the exact same incorrect answer to a problem.

I knew the English teacher to be a thoughtful man who kept a clear head. Indeed, he didn't seem upset or angry in the least when he came to me.

"It's almost certainly cheating. They were all sitting together in the back of the classroom when they took the test. I can talk to them myself, but I thought I should let you know first."

After considering it for a while, I asked if he was willing to let me handle it. If there was cheating going on, it probably wasn't limited to English class.

"Act quickly," he advised. "Let them get away with it once and there will be more students involved when it happens next time."

I took his warning to heart.

I went to the teachers who had these students for other subjects and asked if there had been anything suspicious in the exam answers they'd received. I also reviewed the tests I'd given them in the subjects I taught: social studies and geography.

Despite some similarities in the five students' answers, I could find no clear evidence of cheating in composition, science, or my subjects.

The science teacher's opinion:

"They're not idiots. They wouldn't do anything too obvious. Kids can be crafty when they put their minds to it."

Yet their craftiness failed them when it came to math.

The mathematics teacher:

"A student who doesn't get math in their first or second

year won't suddenly start getting it in their third. I generally know before they take a test which students are going to be able to answer which questions. For example, I know that the final proof on the latest test is beyond Yamaoka's abilities. But look at his answer: 'A D E F.' The correct answer was actually 'Δ D E F.' It's obvious that he looked at someone else's paper and mistook their delta for an A."

It was the sort of elegantly convincing argument you'd expect from a mathematician.

Clearly, I had no reason to be optimistic about the situation, but I had to consider my response. School policy was not to punish students for cheating unless a teacher actually caught them in the act. Yet we had a responsibility to let the students know that we'd noticed what was going on. In other words, to give them a warning. So one day after class, I told the students involved to remain behind.

I told them that they were suspected of cheating, then revealed the reason for our suspicion—that they had all made the exact same mistake on their English exam.

"Well, do any of you have anything to say?" I asked.

No one responded. I singled out Yamaoka and asked again.

He shook his head: "I didn't cheat."

I then asked each of the other students in turn, and all of them denied cheating.

Lacking proof, I couldn't do much more. But they were obviously lying.

All five students looked downcast the whole time I was talking to them, but one in particular, Maeno, was red around his eyes by the time I'd finished. Knowing the students and their previous performances, I was pretty sure that his test had been the source for everyone else's answers. School rules dictated that the one who let his test be copied was just as culpable as those who copied from it.

That night, I received a call from Maeno's mother. She said her son was acting strangely and wondered if anything had happened at school. I told her about the cheating incident, and I could hear her gasp at the other end of the line.

"I suspect your son was the one who showed the others his answers, which unfortunately still counts as cheating. However, because we lack proof of cheating, there won't be any punishment this time. I just gave all five of them a warning. Did your son seem shocked?"

"He came home with his clothes all muddy," she said with tears in her voice. "And now he's locked himself in his room and won't come out. However, I caught a glimpse of his face and it was all swollen, Mr. Kaga. I think he was injured and he might have been bleeding."

The following day, Maeno was out sick. When he came in the day after, he had an eye patch over one eye. The bruises and swelling made it clear someone had beaten him up. I had an idea who.

At this point I finally understood that Maeno wasn't a friend of the students who'd cheated off his test. They'd coerced him into giving them his answers on the test, then pummeled him as punishment for making a mistake that gave them away. At the time, I didn't know whether the bullying had started before the cheating or not.

Soon after this incident, summer vacation started, and the timing couldn't have been worse. Just when I'd opened my eyes to what was going on in my class, they drifted out of my sight. I suppose I could have reached out to them over vacation, but I didn't. I was busy. I had to do a lot of work to help all of my students get into the right high schools in the next half year. I had school pamphlets to gather, and a mountain of recommendations and forms to fill out. But this is just an excuse. Yamaoka and his buddies extorted and stole over a hundred thousand yen—which is a huge amount for a schoolboy—from Maeno over the summer. Even worse than that, the tangled web of power and coercion between them grew ever stronger and more complex. I didn't learn about this until sometime later.

At the beginning of the second semester I became aware, both from a sudden drop in Maeno's grades and because some concerned students confided in me, that the bullying was getting worse, was happening daily. But how bad, I couldn't have imagined. I found out later that Maeno's hair had hid no fewer than six cigarette burns on his scalp.

Some of my colleagues thought that, since the students were about to graduate and go their separate ways, it was best to ignore bullying in the senior class. In other words, let graduation solve the problem. But I didn't feel this was an option. I was still relatively new as a teacher and it was the first year I had a senior class assigned to me for homeroom. I didn't want any of my students to regret having been assigned to my class.

I decided to talk to Maeno first. I wanted to find out how the bullying had started, and what had happened so far.

He refused to talk. Clearly, he was worried that if he did, the bullying would only escalate. From the sweat running down his brow and the trembling in his fingers, I could plainly see the boy was terrified.

I decided the thing to do was to try to improve his

self-confidence. My first idea was kendo. I was in charge of the kendo club at school, and I'd seen many timid young boys take up the sport and transform before my eyes.

As it was a bit late in the year for him to join the kendo club officially, I offered him private lessons in the mornings before school. Though he didn't seem particularly eager, he showed up for those lessons every morning. Maeno was smart enough to realize what I was trying to do.

He took to kendo fairly well, but showed a far keener interest in something else: knife throwing.

I had taken up the practice of knife throwing as a way to help develop focus. The idea is simple enough: throw a knife at a tatami against the wall and try to make it stick. I sometimes threw with my eyes shut, or even with my back turned to the mat. I found that doing this well required absolute concentration—being aware of everything around me, yet maintaining an intense focus on the knife, on its balance, and on the target. To avoid accidents, I always practiced before anyone else showed up at the gym; but Maeno came early one day and saw me. He told me he wanted to try it, too. It was against school rules, letting a student carry or handle an edged weapon such as a knife or sword, so I had to refuse. But I did let him watch me practice. He would stand a safe distance away, a serious look on his face as he studied my movements.

Once he asked me what the trick to it was.

"You just have to believe you can do it," I told him.

Not long after that, Yamaoka, the ringleader of the bullies, was admitted to the hospital for appendicitis. Since I didn't subscribe to the passive route—letting the bullying die out by itself—I saw this as the perfect opportunity to rid Maeno of his feelings of inferiority to Yamaoka.

I told Maeno to copy his class notes and bring them to the hospital every day. With tears in his eyes, he tried to refuse, but I wouldn't hear it. I didn't want to let him graduate feeling like a loser.

I'm not sure what transpired at the hospital. Maeno may silently have put the notes on Yamaoka's bed and left. Maybe the two boys didn't even see each other. I didn't care. As far as I was concerned, as long as Yamaoka felt indebted to Maeno, and Maeno felt empowered, that was good enough.

Shortly after Yamaoka got out of the hospital, I got the confirmation I was looking for that everything was going as I'd planned. I casually asked a few of my students about the state of affairs between Maeno and the gang, and they revealed that the bullying had stopped. Of course the other kids might've been lying, but Maeno was clearly much happier than before, so I decided that things had resolved themselves.

After graduation, I realized just how wrong I was.

On graduation day, I was happy. All of my students were ready to move on to high schools in the area, and they wouldn't be taking any lingering problems with them. Because of my success that year, I was starting to feel some confidence in my choice of profession.

Then that night I received a phone call from the police. The officer in charge of juvenile affairs said something that made my blood run cold: Maeno had been arrested on charges of battery and assault with a deadly weapon. He had stabbed Yamaoka at a local video arcade.

At first, I thought the officer got it wrong. Wasn't it the other way around?

It turned out both boys were injured. At the time of his arrest, Maeno's clothes were ripped, the side of his face was swollen, and he was bruised all over.

After graduation, Yamaoka and his cronies had found Maeno alone and ganged up on him. They'd only been holding off while they were still in school because of that nosy teacher, Mr. Kaga. But as soon as they were beyond my reach, they beat Maeno to a bloody pulp and pissed on his face.

I don't know how long Maeno lay there, bloodied and bruised, after he was beaten. But the first thing he did after he struggled to his feet was head for the kendo room in the gym. There, he broke into my locker and took one of my throwing knives.

He knew where Yamaoka would be because over the past year they'd forced him to bring them money there time and time again. When he found them at the arcade, he didn't hesitate. He went straight to Yamaoka and stabbed him, again and again.

The arcade owner called the police. When they arrived, Maeno was just standing there, my knife still in his hand.

I went to the police station right away, but Maeno refused to see me. I did learn, however, that Yamaoka would recover, that his wounds were not fatal.

The next day, the officer in charge of the case told me, "You know, Maeno was ready to die in that video arcade after stabbing that kid. I asked the other kids involved why they'd beaten Maeno up in the first place, and they said it was because they didn't like him. When I asked why they didn't like him, do you know what they said? 'Just because.'"

Those words devastated me.

I never spoke to either Maeno or Yamaoka again. According to Maeno's mother, who did speak to me briefly after the incident, I was "the last person in the world" Maeno wanted to see.

When April came around and it was time for a new school year to start, I didn't have it in me to return to the classroom. So I fled. To this day, I believe that my actions that year constitute the greatest failure of my life.

9

TRUTH

KYOICHIRO KAGA'S SOLUTION

How are you feeling? I spoke to the doctor before coming in here, and he tells me you've decided to go through with the surgery. I was relieved to hear that. You've signed all the permission forms and they're ready to go ahead. So there's no turning back now. Apparently, there's a fairly high chance of success, too. I'm not telling you that to make you feel better. It's the truth.

"I want to ask you, when did you first realize you were sick? Was it this winter? This year?

"No, I'm guessing you knew the cancer had returned by the end of last year at the latest. And you thought this time might be the last go-around. That there would be no remissions or second chances. Am I right? That's why you didn't bother going to the hospital?

"I have a reason for believing this. I think that's when you started planning Kunihiko Hidaka's murder.

"Surprised? You shouldn't be. There's a logical basis for my assertion. I even have evidence. That's what I wanted to talk to you about this afternoon. I might be here a little longer than usual today, but don't worry, your doctor has given me permission.

"Take a look at this. Recognize this image? It's from the video of you sneaking into Hidaka's house. The one Hidaka supposedly made by setting up a hidden camera in his garden, catching you in the act. According to your confession, that is.

"If you'd like, I can bring a player in here and we can review the whole video, but I don't think that'll be necessary. This one frame will be enough. Besides, you're probably sick of seeing that footage, right? After all, you staged it, you performed it, and you filmed it. It was your directorial and acting debut.

"Yes, I am claiming it's a fake. Everything on this tape is a lie. That's what I'm going to prove to you now, using this photograph. See, this video wasn't filmed seven years ago, like the date in the bottom purports.

"Let me explain. It's very simple. We can see Hidaka's garden here, right? Notice the plants. I realize there aren't many in this image. The famous cherry tree is just outside the frame, and the lawn is withered. You can tell at a glance that this was taken during the winter. Not *that* winter. Just *a* winter. That, and since it was taken in the middle of the night, it's too dark to make out much detail. I suppose that's why you thought it would fool us.

"Mr. Nonoguchi, unfortunately you made a big mistake. No, I'm not bluffing, you really did make a mistake. See this blotch across the lawn here? That's the shadow of the cherry tree, cast by a streetlamp out at the road. It's faint, yes, but it's fatal to your subterfuge.

"I know, I know. The quality of the video and the way the light shines into the garden make it hard to determine whether this is the cherry tree of seven years or only half a year ago. On that account, you're perfectly correct. But that's not what I wanted to point out. The problem here isn't the shape of the shadow, it's that there's only one tree.

"You seem confused, so let me explain. If this video really was taken in the Hidakas' garden seven years ago, there would have to be two shadows across the lawn here. Do you know why? Because seven years ago, there were two cherry trees in the Hidakas' garden standing side by side. A lovely couple.

"So, no, the video wasn't recorded years ago. It was taken recently, and it was taken by you. Rie Hidaka seems to think it wouldn't have been difficult for you to stage your video shoot toward the end of last year. Kunihiko Hidaka was still single at the time, she hadn't yet moved into the house, and all you would've had to do was wait for a night when he was out drinking with one of his editors.

"Of course, you'd need a key to the house to make sure the office window was unlocked. It wouldn't have made such a great video if you weren't able to climb in the window for your big 'murder attempt.' Oh, I know you didn't have a set of keys to Hidaka's house. Rie didn't think that would've been problematic, either, though. When her late husband went out drinking, he never took his keys with him. Ever since he lost his keys once while out on the town, he'd taken to hiding them behind the flower pot outside the front door. As long as you knew that, you wouldn't need your own set of keys. Rie is fairly sure that was something you did know.

"I can guess what you're thinking, Mr. Nonoguchi. *What detective analyzes every little shadow in a videotape on the off chance something might not correspond to the vegetation present seven years ago in a garden?* Well, you're right. No one does that, not even me. See, it wasn't the lack of an extra tree that made me realize the videotape was a fake. Rather, it was because I *knew* the tape was a fake that I watched it over and over again, going so far as to hunt down the one or two extant photos of the Hi-dakas' garden in order to find the evidence I needed. But how did I know it was a fake? Because another piece of evidence from your confession was called into question: namely, the giant pile of manuscripts found in your apartment. The ones I was sure were connected to your motive for murdering Hidaka.

"There were several things that struck me as odd when I read the confession you wrote following your arrest. It was possible to explain each away individually, but taken together, they gave me the impression there was something else at work in your account, Mr. Nonoguchi. There was an insincerity running through it that made me unable to simply accept what you'd written as the truth.

"That was when I found my first big clue. I was amazed that, given the number of times I'd met with you, I hadn't no-ticed it before. It was staring me in the face the whole time.

"Mr. Nonoguchi, please hold out your right hand. Just your fingers will do. Note the pen callus on your middle fin-ger. It's quite thick.

"But that's odd, isn't it? You don't write longhand, you use a word processor for your stories. You also used it for your re-ports and so forth you wrote back when you worked as a teacher. So why did you have such a large pen callus? Perhaps you'd like me to believe it's *not* a pen callus. Then what is it? You don't know? You can't remember anything that could have caused that bump on your finger?

"Don't worry about it too much. The only thing that's im-portant here is that, to me, it looked like a pen callus. And the only reason for someone who uses a word processor to have such a nice thick pen callus would be because he'd recently needed to write a very large quantity of material by hand.

"That got me thinking. And let me tell you, what I came up with sent a chill down my spine. If my new theory was correct, it meant that my investigation would take a full one-hundred-and-eighty-degree turn.

"I'll cut to the chase: all those manuscripts found in your apartment were not written over the last couple of decades, they weren't written back in high school or college, but instead they were written very recently, in great haste. Chilling, I know. Because that would mean that Mr. Hidaka hadn't stolen your work, or stolen any ideas from those manuscripts at all.

"But a theory without proof isn't enough. I needed some way to prove it, so I did some looking around.

"Mr. Nonoguchi, do you know a man by the name of Heikichi Tsujimura? You don't? I didn't think so.

"In your confession, you wrote that as children you and Kunihiko Hidaka used to go watch the neighborhood fire-works maker at work. You said that it was your memory of these occasions that formed the basis for your story *A Circle of Fire,* the very story on which Mr. Hidaka based his novel *An Unburning Flame.*

"That fireworks maker's name was Mr. Tsujimura. Yes, of course you might've simply forgotten the name. That's not important. I imagine that, had I been able to ask Kunihiko Hidaka if he remembered, it's possible he might've forgotten, too.

"But Mr. Tsujimura—who, by the way, is still alive; over ninety and in a wheelchair, but sharp as a tack—hadn't forgotten the boy who came to visit. One boy, not two. I showed him your middle-school yearbook and he pointed out the boy's face right away: Kunihiko Hidaka.

"Oh, and when I showed him your face, he said he'd never seen you before.

"It was his testimony that removed my last remaining shred of doubt. Mr. Hidaka hadn't stolen your work, hadn't based any of his novels on your writings. All those manuscripts were stories and novels derived by you, closely based on his books. Then I started working backward from that fact, the fact that he didn't plagiarize a word from you. If there was no plagiarism, then there was no blackmail, and if not blackmail, ultimately, no attempted murder.

"What are we to make, then, of your alleged relationship to Hatsumi Hidaka, the supposed motive for your attempted murder? Was there really an infidelity, as you claimed? Let's review the evidence.

"First we have the apron, the necklace, and the travel documents found in your apartment. Next we have the photograph, discovered later, of Hatsumi, taken at what appears to be the Fuji River rest area. Not to mention the photo of Mount Fuji taken from the same spot.

"That's it. There was nothing else. Nor were there any witnesses who could testify to seeing the two of you alone together, much less testify to a relationship between you.

"Of these, the travel documents could have been written up at any time, so they prove nothing. Furthermore, the necklace you claimed was a present for Hatsumi could've been for anyone, or no one at all. The apron, however, does appear to have been Hatsumi's apron. As I told you before, we found a photograph of her wearing it.

"However, it would've been a rather simple task for you to steal an apron out of Hidaka's house, possibly on one of those nights when he was out drinking with an editor or perhaps when you went to help him clean out his deceased wife's belongings before he married Rie.

"On that same occasion, you could've stolen a photograph. Specifically, one that fulfilled the following conditions: it had to show Hatsumi standing alone, and there needed to be no other photographs showing Kunihiko in the same place. Another photograph showing something innocuous, like a view from the same place, would be the icing on the cake. The photograph meeting all of those conditions was the one taken at the Fuji River rest area.

"No, of course I have no proof you stole anything. I'm merely saying it was possible. But, given the number of times I've been misled by things you've written, the mere possibility is enough to convince me I shouldn't accept the details of your alleged relationship with Hatsumi at face value.

"Of course, if there was no attempted murder, no blackmail, and no plagiarism, then it would only stand to reason that the precondition necessary for all of those events to take place—Hatsumi's adultery—also did not occur. This also clears up the matter of Hatsumi's accidental death. It was simply that: an accident. There was no motive for suicide.

"Let's take a look at what we have so far—specifically, what you've been up to since fall of last year. I'll try to keep things in chronological order.

"First, you procured some unused, but old—and old-looking—spiral notebooks. I'm sure you were able to find them stashed somewhere in the school where you taught. Then, you began copying Kunihiko Hidaka's published works. Not exact copies, because you adjusted them to give the impression that these were the originals upon which those published works had been based. I'd guess it took you something on the order of a full month to rewrite each novel. That must've been quite a chore. For the newer works, of course, you simply used your word processor. The stories written on composition paper that were without counterparts in Hidaka's published works were things that you actually did write back in your college days.

"As for *The Gates of Ice*, this is where we really see the hand of the master planner. Anticipating events, you realized you needed story memos for the detectives to find, and you needed to have written the next installment to use as your alibi when you killed Hidaka.

"Then comes the video. As I said, you probably took this toward the end of last year. Then, in the new year, you obtained Hatsumi's apron and photograph. No doubt you also filled out those travel forms and bought the necklace around the same time. Did you already have blank travel forms lying around? Maybe you found those at your school, too. Also, you claimed that the paisley necktie in your dresser was from Hatsumi, and the teacup in the cupboard was one you had purchased together. You probably picked up both of these items rather recently and by yourself.

"Next we come to a very important final step. I hear that it took the Hidakas about a week to prepare all of their things to send to Canada, during which time you visited their house once. I believe your main goal for this visit was to conceal two items in their luggage: the knife and the videotape. The tape you placed inside a hollowed-out copy of Hidaka's book in order to create the impression that it was something he'd been hiding.

"Then you waited until April sixteenth, the day you murdered Kunihiko Hidaka.

"Clearly this wasn't a momentary loss of control or an act carried out 'in the heat of the moment.' It was a terrifyingly premeditated execution, the result of a great deal of planning. While you put an impressive amount of thought and energy into it, this alone doesn't distinguish your crime from all the other murders. I have to admit, the twist you put on it was genius. Typically, much of the planning that goes into a premeditated murder involves schemes to establish an alibi, avoid arrest, or, at the very least, avoid blame.

"But your plan was unique. You had an entirely different goal in mind. You wanted to get arrested. You didn't care about committing the perfect crime. You wanted to establish the perfect motive.

"I know. It's a rather startling idea. You may be the first murderer that decided to fabricate a motive before committing the crime. Believe me, I almost couldn't bring myself to accept the truth. During the long hours it took me to reach the point where I was confident I'd uncovered the truth, I doubted myself every step of the way. In fact, I refused to believe what the facts were telling me.

"Of course, had we questioned any of the evidence earlier— say, the videotape—then we might well have resolved this much more quickly. Yet who would suspect a killer of forging a vital piece of evidence indicating his own guilt of a crime? Truly, that was a brilliant stroke.

"The same goes for the fake manuscripts you prepared

and the clues you planted suggesting that you had had a relationship with Hatsumi Hidaka. If any of those had been evidence that exonerated you, we would have certainly put them under a microscope. Yet we did nothing of the sort because every bit of it seemed to only confirm your motive. It is an unfortunate fact that the police tend to turn a stern eye toward evidence that benefits a suspect, but tend to be rather easygoing when it comes to evidence that implicates our suspect. A tendency you deftly took advantage of.

"You led our investigation down the exact wrong path with a series of carefully laid traps. The first was the notebooks you prepared. The second was the apron, the necklace, the travel documents, and the photograph of Hatsumi Hidaka. Thinking back on it, I suspect you were getting nervous when it took us so long to find that photograph. That's probably why you felt the need to drop that hint about the 'important books.' How relieved you must have been when I took the bait.

"I required a little guidance to fall into the third trap as well. If you hadn't gone out of your way to ask Rie about the tapes Hidaka sent to Canada, I might never have keyed in to their importance. You must have been so pleased with your idea to hide the tape inside a copy of *Sea Ghost*—the novel that inspired your false motive in the first place. You even made sure I was aware of that particular novel by recommending it to me the first night we met. That was all part of your plan, too, wasn't it? I have to say, I'm impressed.

"Now let's turn back the hands of the clock just a touch further to the day you killed Kunihiko Hidaka.

"The murder was planned quite thoroughly, yet you couldn't have anyone catching on to that fact. It had to seem like a rash act done out of desperation, in the 'heat of the moment.' Anything else would undermine your false motive. A knife or poison wouldn't work, those would be too obviously premeditated. What about strangulation? Considering your relative physical strengths, that might be difficult for you to accomplish.

"No, your best bet was blunt trauma: striking him with a dull instrument from behind. Once he'd fallen to the floor you could easily strangle him. But you'd still need a suitable murder weapon—one that you could have found at the scene. Hidaka's paperweight would do the trick nicely. How to strangle him? A telephone cord! I can just picture you checking off each item on your mental checklist.

"Here, however, was a potential problem. The movers having already packed up most of the house, what if the paperweight was no longer there? Unlike the phone cord, the paperweight wasn't an absolute necessity. It could already be packed in some cardboard box.

"So you prepared a backup: the Dom Pérignon. The bottle was intended as your backup murder weapon, which is why you didn't offer the gift upon your arrival. If you did, they might store it somewhere out of easy reach. No, first you had to check the office. Relieved to see that the paperweight was still there, you were then free to give them the champagne bottle as a gift to celebrate their big move.

"When I first heard about the champagne, I wondered if it had been poisoned. I even asked the manager of the hotel who ended up with it how it tasted. He said it was quite good. Of course, now I know that you never would've used poison in the first place.

"The trick you used to establish your alibi—using the fax software on the computer—was brilliant. Smart enough to fool an older detective—I'm pretty sure the chief still hasn't figured it out, by the way—and yet flawed enough, with the monitor left on and the wrong redial number on the house phone, that someone was sure to see through it.

"I wonder what you would have done if we hadn't figured it out, though. What if you were never even a suspect? I see you're hesitant to respond. Well, don't worry about it. We did see through your trick, as intended, and you *were* arrested.

"You look tired. I'm sorry to have talked for so long. But bear with me just a little longer. After all, you put me through quite a lot to reach this point. It seems only fair that you suffer a little yourself.

"Let's get down to the big question here: Why go through all that trouble to construct a false motive with the express intent of being arrested? It flies in the face of common sense.

"Of course you had a motive, a different motive, for killing Kunihiko Hidaka. And you were more frightened that your true motive would be revealed than you were of being found guilty for the murder of Kunihiko Hidaka.

"As for what that motive was, I know what it is, but I'd really like to hear it from you. Well? Why not tell me? I can't see that there's any point in you remaining silent.

"No? Very well. As you seem to have no intention of talking, let me tell you instead.

"Do know what this is, Mr. Nonoguchi? That's right, a CD. Not for music. It's a CD-ROM, one Hidaka had burned for himself. It turns out that several years ago, he started keeping all his research materials—photos included—on CD. He scanned his older photos and starting using a digital camera to take the newer ones.

"Why did I think to look through all of Hidaka's reference photos? It was because, in the course of sorting through the past—his past, and your past—a particular photograph came to my attention. If that photograph showed what I thought it might, then something I hadn't been paying much attention to would suddenly become extremely important, and several unrelated facts would line up quite nicely.

"It turns out that the original photograph had already been thrown away. But I knew that Mr. Hidaka had had it in his possession and had plenty of time to make a copy. Thus, this CD. Sorry, I know I'm being overly dramatic, building up to this; but there really isn't any need, is there? You already know what photo I mean. It's an old Polaroid of Masaya Fujio assaulting a middle-school girl.

"The photograph's quite clear. I was going to print it out and bring it with me but there really wasn't any point. You know what I saw in that photograph. It was exactly what I'd anticipated. You were the one holding her down, Mr. Nonoguchi. You helped Masaya Fujio rape that girl.

"I looked into your days in middle school and I heard a lot of different things from a lot of different people. The subject of bullying came up quite a bit. Some said you were a victim. Others said you were one of the bullies yourself. I think both statements are correct. You were bullied and continued to be bullied even when you joined Fujio's circle. Only the form that the bullying took changed as you went along.

"From your experience as a teacher, you know as well as I do that bullying never ends. As long as the people involved are at the same school, it keeps going on. When a teacher says, 'There's no more bullying in my class,' what they're really saying is 'I'd like to believe there's no more bullying in my class.'

"I realize what happened to that girl left a very deep scar on you. I don't believe you did what you did willingly, or that you took any joy in it. You simply knew that if you turned against Masaya Fujio, you'd be back in hell. When I think about the guilt you must have felt, the self-loathing, I feel physical pain, Mr. Nonoguchi, and I wasn't even there. That day was the last time you were bullied, and probably the worst.

"You wanted more than anything to bury that dark memory in the past. You wanted it so much, you were willing to kill for it.

"But wait.

"Why did this secret start bothering you now? Hidaka had obtained the photograph before he wrote *Forbidden Hunting Grounds*, and there was no sign that he had shown it to anyone afterward. Why couldn't you assume that your secret was safe with him?

"Please don't try to tell me that Hidaka was using that photograph to blackmail you. The same lie won't work twice; and besides, it's simply beneath the architect of such a masterful crime.

"I suspect Miyako Fujio threw a wrench into everything. She was ready to take Kunihiko Hidaka to court over what he wrote in his book, specifically the thinly disguised portrait of her brother. Hidaka, meanwhile, had begun to realize it might be inevitable. That got you worrying. What would you do if that photograph was submitted as evidence in court?

"I imagine your worries began when Hidaka wrote that

novel. When Ms. Fujio started pressing Hidaka, your fear built until, finally, you were ready to commit murder.

"That sounds plausible. Except, I've left out the most important piece of the puzzle: the true nature of your relationship with Kunihiko Hidaka. Why did you feel the need to kill Hidaka to keep your secret? This was a man who you were on friendly terms with in recent years. He never even alluded to you or what you did in his novel about Fujio. Why couldn't you expect Hidaka to continue to keep your secret safe even if things got drawn out between him and Miyako Fujio?

"In your confession, you portrayed the relationship between Hidaka and Ms. Fujio as one of mutual antagonism. Yet we owe it to ourselves to question everything you've written, don't you agree? Let's look at some facts we were able to independently corroborate. One, you weren't friends with Hidaka in middle school, yet you actively sought out his friendship and indeed established a relationship with him years later. He even helped introduce you to a publisher so you could become a full-time writer, writing children's books. Furthermore, in his repeated talks with Miyako Fujio, your name and your involvement in the events described in *Forbidden Hunting Grounds* remained a secret, again due to Hidaka's discretion.

"If we try to reconstruct who Hidaka was from just these facts, we find he closely resembles himself as a child. 'A boy who was kind to everyone around him,' as he's been described. In fact, I think it's possible that, regardless of your intentions, Hidaka honestly thought of you as a friend.

"It took me some time to arrive at this realization because this image of Hidaka was so different than the one I had as I began the investigation. In fact, that image tugged at the back of my mind the entire time I was gathering information about Hidaka's childhood days.

"Was this disjuncture between what I was hearing and what I felt the result of what I read in your false confession? No. The negative image of Hidaka had been planted in my head much earlier than that—before your arrest. Ultimately I realized where it came from: your original account of the day of the murder.

"When I first read that account, I paid attention only to the details about the discovery of the body itself. Yet there was a very deeply laid trap in the last place I thought to look for one.

"From the look on your face, I can tell I've hit the mark. That's right, I'm talking about the cat. The one you killed.

We found the pesticide mixed into the dirt in the planters at your apartment. You would have been better off flushing the extra down the drain. The pesticide in your apartment matched the one we found in the cat. The owner had it in a box and buried it in her garden. Yes, we exhumed the cat and tested the body.

"Maybe you read about Hidaka's trouble with that cat in his article? Or since you two were getting along so well, maybe he told you himself? So you made the poisoned meatballs, snuck into the garden, and killed that woman's cat, all to support an image of Hidaka you intended to craft in my mind.

"You know, once I realized I'd be spending time in the literary world while on this case, I decided to do a little background reading. That's when I came across the concept of establishing character. Apparently, it won't do just to tell the reader what a particular character is like. The author needs to show their habits or their words and let the reader form an image on their own.

"So, when you started writing your first account, you already knew you'd need to establish your main character, Kunihiko Hidaka, as early as possible. What better way to show his cruelty than to have him kill a cat? What a happy coincidence you ran into the cat's owner in the garden that day. Throwing that in at the beginning of your account just made the revelation of Hidaka's wrongdoing all the more believable.

"I fell for it, hook, line, and sinker. Even after I'd arrested you and realized that your account wasn't to be trusted, it never occurred to me that the episode with the cat might be a lie, and I never attempted to adjust my initial impression of Hidaka.

"I believe that of all the traps you laid for me, that was your finest.

"When I realized it was you who killed the cat, a lightbulb went on. What if the reason you killed the cat was the same reason for the entire crime? In other words, what if your real objective was not just to kill Hidaka, but to ruin him? *Now,* I thought, *we're getting somewhere.*

"Just a moment ago I suggested that you wanted to cover up your own past by killing the only one who knew about it. You made no attempt to deny this, and I think there's some truth to this. But it wasn't the reason for your elaborate plan, it was just the final push you needed.

"Once you decided Hidaka had to die, what were your next steps? The first thing you realized was that you'd need a proper motive. It would have to be one that would, once revealed, not only defame the actual victim but would also turn public sympathy in your favor. The solution you came up started with his wife Hatsumi's infidelity and ended with your enforced ghostwriting. If everything went according to plan, not only would you destroy Hatsumi's reputation and Hidaka's character, but you'd forever blacken his professional reputation and steal the credit for his writing to boot.

"This, of course, was the prize you were working for as you wrote out all of those manuscripts and spent those hours under the cold winter sky making your video. I doubt you'd have gone to such lengths merely to hide your own past. That was worth a little effort, sure, but murder was just another step in your plan to destroy everything Hidaka ever built and taint everything he ever had.

"I wondered for a long time what it would take to drive someone to do that. To devote what little time remained to them to destroying another person's character. To be honest, I couldn't find any logical explanation for such behavior. I wonder if you'd even be able to explain it yourself, Mr. Nonoguchi.

"It reminds me of something that happened ten years ago. Perhaps you remember—that time when one of my students stabbed the ringleader of a group of bullies right after graduation. When the police asked those bullies why they'd abused my student so severely, all they were able to come up with was that they 'just didn't like him.' It was just hate. Pure, simple malice.

"I wonder if you aren't operating on the same level. I wonder if, deep inside you, it wasn't just malice toward Hidaka, incomprehensible even to yourself, that led to his death.

"But where could such malice have come from? I looked

into your past and his in great detail, but I couldn't find any reason why Hidaka earned your hatred. He was a good boy . . . no, an exceptional boy. You should have thanked him, not killed him. Even after you'd spent all that time egging on Masaya Fujio, goading him to torture Hidaka, years later he was there to help you.

"I know you felt inferior to him. And I know how, as an adult, you envied Hidaka. The one person in the world you couldn't bear had become a hugely successful author. Everything you wanted, he'd achieved. When I imagine how you must've felt when he received his first award, it makes all the hair on my body stand on end.

"But you still reached out to him, didn't you? That's how badly you wanted to become a published author. You thought having a connection to him would be a shortcut to achieving your dream, so you decided to ignore the malice in your heart, if only temporarily.

"It wasn't easy, was it? I can't say whether it was bad luck, a lack of talent, or a mix of both, but you never realized your dream. When your body began to fall apart around you, you realized that you never would.

"When you realized your own death was imminent, you stopped holding back. You couldn't bear to leave this world with so much rage burning inside you. The fact that Hidaka knew about your past and he had proof that could expose those secrets, that wasn't the reason you acted. But it was enough to push you over the edge, to push that darkness you held within you out into the light. You decided to spend your last days planning the perfect crime. You murdered a man and let yourself get caught in order to steal everything from your victim—to ruin his name and his honor and everything he loved, even stealing the credit for the books he wrote.

"That pretty much sums up my thoughts on this case. Do you disagree with anything I've said? . . . I'll take your silence as a no.

"Let me suggest one last thing before I go.

"In the background interviews I conducted, people remember you and your mother having a dislike, even a prejudice, against Hidaka and the other people living in your neighborhood.

"There was no basis for that prejudice. Nor any indication anyone else shared that prejudice.

"It occurred to me that this whole dislike of Hidaka might not have started with you at all. It might be your mother's misguided prejudices that planted the seed that led you astray. I just wanted you to know that. Since you can't blame Hidaka anymore, maybe you can blame her.

"I've been talking for some time, haven't I? My mouth's quite dry.

"Now that you've given your permission for the surgery— and I checked, it's irrevocable—the doctors will be coming for you soon. I hope your surgery is a success, and that you have many years left ahead of you.

"After all, you have a trial to look forward to."